ENIGMATIC THREADS OF FATE

When our souls entangled

Jiya & Joy Sengal

BLUEROSE PUBLISHERS
India | U.K.

Copyright © Jiya and Joy Sengal 2023

All rights reserved by author. No part of this publication may be reproduced, stored in a retrieval system or transmitted in any form or by any means, electronic, mechanical, photocopying, recording or otherwise, without the prior permission of the author. Although every precaution has been taken to verify the accuracy of the information contained herein, the publisher assumes no responsibility for any errors or omissions. No liability is assumed for damages that may result from the use of information contained within.

BlueRose Publishers takes no responsibility for any damages, losses, or liabilities that may arise from the use or misuse of the information, products, or services provided in this publication.

For permissions requests or inquiries regarding this publication, please contact:

BLUEROSE PUBLISHERS
www.BlueRoseONE.com
info@bluerosepublishers.com
+91 8882 898 898
+4407342408967

ISBN: 978-93-5819-202-5

Typesetting: Pooja Sharma

First Edition: September 2023

Prologue

The sun was rising over the horizon, casting a warm glow on the city with its vibrant yellow hues. People were rushing to their work, while the streets came alive with the noise of vehicles. Locals gathered at a café to embrace the enriching taste of freshly brewed coffee.

In the midst of all the chaos, she seemed to have found her moments of peace. She was taking a walk in the garden close to her apartment, occasionally taking pictures of life's fleeting moments. She had an enchanting smile, an adventurous soul finding joy in the simple things of life. While she was lost in her own world, she had no idea that their paths would cross unexpectedly, as if fate already wrote what awaits her.

Suddenly, his eyes fell on her, the dreamy eye stole his attention as if he found solace in them. Her eyes were full of stories that remain unwritten – someone who yearned to unravel the mysteries of life. Soon she noticed he was looking at her, their eyes remain locked for a moment as if they said it all without even using words. He was captivated by her presence. And then he immediately took his eyes off her, pretending he didn't look.

He was totally captivated by her presence, and unable to contain the excitement, he approached her and expressed what he felt about her – although he met her for the first time it seemed as if they had known each other for a longer while. As if fate already weaved the threads that connected them in some way.

She laughed as she heard that, and soon they found themselves talking about their dreams and everyday life. They started to enjoy each other's company.

That was the moment when it all began. They didn't spoke for a while, he walked away with his heart beating faster than usual as if each beat was yearning for the answer of the one question, who was she?

You never know how we meet people in our life unexpectedly and over time they become a part our life – something inseparable, but what about the havoc of emotions we experience when they're gone? How can we be strangers with someone with whom we made a lot of memories? What if their memories keep coming back to us?

How about looking for the same old person in the words we read or the songs that we listen to? we've all experienced that, haven't we? we keep looking for the same person in every person we meet. We all have felt that words are not enough and yet we all have tried to convey our feeling whether it's a warm embrace in their arms, walking along side with our fingers entwined, coming up with words to write a single line that summarises our love for them.

Although their first interaction contained very few words and yet each word of her had a deeper meaning, as if she was the book and he only read the first page. But that was enough to evoke a sense of curiosity – hoping he would get to meet her again. We're all waiting for someone to tap into the chapters of our life, dive deep into the words and make sense of them in their own unique ways.

But she was more like a favourite book in the shelf. You don't know how it would turn out when you pick it up, soon as you start reading, it becomes your favourite. You keep going back to certain phrases of it – even when you're not reading.

Contents

Book 1: Weaving Stories 1

   Chapter – 1 2

   Chapter – 2 25

Book 2: Chasing Memories 41

   Chapter – 3 42

   Chapter – 4 60

Book 3: Shattered Promises 78

   Chapter – 5 79

   Chapter – 6 100

Book 4: Embracing Dreams 112

   Chapter – 7 113

   Chapter – 8 127

Book 5: Faded Memories 136

   Chapter – 9 137

   Chapter – 10 149

Book 6: Whispered Feelings 165

   Chapter – 11 166

   Chapter – 12 184

Book 7: Everlasting Love 207
    Chapter – 13 208
    Chapter – 14 226
Epilogue 232
About The Author 236

Book 1: Weaving Stories

Chapter – 1

April 2023, Ahmedabad

It was 8 in the morning, the city had already woken up, workers were rushing to catch their train, bakery and coffee shops were emitting a beautiful aroma. In her apartment, Priya was still asleep, she wasn't a morning person. Her room was enveloped in chilly ambience of the air conditioner, 17-degree temperature was enough to give her a cosy and peaceful sleep.

Her mother slowly opened the door, and the chill of the room caught her off guard, causing her to shiver. She walked over to the window and slid the curtains all over to the end, allowing the morning sunlight to illuminate the room. She noticed the bed of her daughter, who was still lost in her deep slumber, immersed in her imagined world of dreams.

"Priya," she whispered, her voice a gentle voice. While caressing her hairs.

Priya slowly opened her eyes as she felt the warm touch of her mother.

"Good morning, mom," She said as she took a deep breath.

"Good morning, my dear," her mother said, her voice filled with affection.

Why don't you make it a habit to wake up early. you know we have somewhere to go, she said as she caressed her hand on Priya's head.

"Don't worry mom, I'll be ready in no time." Priya said, she turned off the air conditioner.

Priya's parents had planned to meet a family to talk about her wedding with their son.

Priya stepped out from the bed and went to the bathroom to freshen up, she immediately splashed water which awakened her senses after a deep sleep. She noticed the clock; she was already getting late. Priya went to the bathroom to take a quick shower and then she wore her favourite outfit.

He mother had prepared simple yet nourishing breakfast for Priya allowing her a fresh start of the day. While she was having her breakfast her father broke the silence.

"He is 3 years younger than you, which I think you should be aware of." Her

"I don't have any issues with that," Priya said as she was busy grabbing her bite.

Her mother seemed to be upset about that, she remained quiet for a while, expressing her disagreement. She was worried about what others would say after learning about this.

In the midst of the conversation, Priya took a moment to think. She longed for a bond that would resonate deeply with her. Someone who would walk alongside her through the highs and lows of life. Her heart whispered for a love that encompass the depths of joy and vulnerability of life, someone who would envelop her in the comfortable warm embrace in her low moments, someone with whom she could simply entangle her soul and enrich every moment they would experience in life – weaving stories that would sail across the tides of love forever.

She completed her breakfast and rushed to the parking of her apartment; she immediately stepped into her car feeling a sense of excitement. As she navigated the busy streets of Ahmedabad, her heart was filled with anticipation for what life had in store for her.

Priya arrived at the coffee shop sooner than expected, she parked her car with a rush of emotions, she took a deep breath as she approached the door preparing herself for the meeting. She stepped inside the coffee shop; the aroma of the freshly brewed coffee enveloped the ambience.

she looked around, trying to notice someone sitting alone. she saw his picture on her father's phone so she could easily recognise him, but he wasn't there yet. She took a table and calmed herself down, she didn't order anything except a glass of water.

A familiar face opened the door of the café and stepped inside, the aroma of fresh coffee enveloped him and awakened his senses, his heart raced with anticipation as he was searching for her.

And there she was, sitting alone at a table close to the window, lost in her own thoughts. Her radiant smiled was lighting up the mood around her. she looked even more beautiful than he imagined. Her sparkling eyes were enough to captivate him. He collected his thoughts for a moment and took a deep breath and then he started walking his way towards her. his mind kept rehearsing the words he was going to say to her and the way he'd express his feelings towards her.

He seemed as nervous as she was, which made her smile, his nervous was apparent on his face. She pretended as if she didn't notice him and to her surprise, he soon approached the table. He sat beside her, their eyes locked for a moment, feeling a surge of excitement and nervousness at the same time.

"Hey, I'm so glad you came here." He smiled as he said that, as if the smile brought him a little relief.

"Hey" she said and looked away from him for a moment to collect her thoughts.

The waiter approached them asking for the order, "What can I get you?" He said in a pleasant and comfortable manner.

"Two coffees please," said Priya, as she looked at him.

The waiter went to the kitchen to prepare two cups of coffee for them.

"By the way, I'm Ajay," he introduced himself, extending his hand for a handshake.

"Priya," she said, as they shook their hands.

"So, I've heard from my parents that you're moving to Canada?" She asked still feeling a bit of nervousness.

"My uncle owns a company over there and he's offering me a position of a director." He said

"That's great," She said

"Thank you. You know what, I think that if doing what you love makes you happy, then who cares what people think. We cannot restrict our happiness just for the sake of what others would say," He said as a surge or confidence rushed over him.

"I agree with you," She said.

They continued chatting for a while, talking about their daily life and wondering what life had in store for them. The earlier clouds of nervousness seemed to have faded away, they were more comfortable in each other's presence.

"Can I ask you something personal?" he inquired.

"Sure," she said, curious about the question he was about to ask.

"Have you ever been in a relationship?" he asked.

"No, I haven't," she said with a smile. "I haven't met anyone with whom I felt ready to commit to a relationship." She said, "What about you?"

"Honestly, I've been in two relationships, but it seems like life had other plans for me," He said

As they were talking, Ajay's phone rang, it was from his father. He picked it up, his father informed him about another girl he had to meet, after meeting Priya.

As Ajay disconnected the call, Priya immediately asked him, "Is everything okay?"

Ajay hesitated for a moment, then decided to share the news. "My father just informed me that I have to meet someone else right after our meeting." he looked a bit disappointed.

Priya thought for a moment, and then she said, "You know what? Maybe we should spend some more time together. It seems what we know about each other is just the surface stuff. Let's make the most of our time and get to know more about each other."

"Sounds like a great idea," his face lightened up as he said that.

Soon after, they left the cafe after spending some time in each other's company and developing their bond.

Sitting in the car, they arrived at the riverfront together. As they made their way to the riverfront, they talked incessantly about their likes and dislikes.

"My friends and I often spend some time over here, usually at the evening after a hectic day we find ourselves enveloped in the comfort of this place," she said.

Ajay couldn't help but smile.

"Maybe we should meet each other more often," she said, making it obvious that she wanted to further their connection and cultivate a bond.

"Sure, would you like to go somewhere?" He asked his voice filled with anticipation.

"How about Goa?" She asked out of curiosity; she knew she wasn't serious about Goa.

"Sounds like a plan, we should arrange a trip to Goa for a few days." he said, a hint of excitement in his voice.

"Are you serious?" she said unable to contain her laughter.

"Of course, I am." He said

Just as they were discussing their plans about Goa, Priya's friend approached her with her lively dog, the friendly pup couldn't contain the excitement and started playing with Priya.

"He's adorable, isn't he?" Priya said as she was caressing the back of the dog.

"I can't see your friends anywhere, aren't they with you?" Asked Priya's friend

"Oh no, actually they're still at work and couldn't make it," Priya said feeling a bit disappointment, "But hey, let me introduce you to my friend Ajay." She said

Ajay extended his hand as a friendly gesture, excited to meet new people.

"It's a pleasure to meet you." Ajay said with a warm smile.

Ajay joined in the fun, slowly reaching his hand to touch the dog on its back, the dog sniffed Ajay's hand and started playing with him.

"I'm getting late Priya, see you later." And then Priya's friend walked away with her dog who was still in the mood to play.

"I would really love to get a pet like that," she said with an innocent smile.

"I can get you one," he said.

They kept looking at each other for a while, and then he broke the eye contact. "Let's go somewhere else," He said.

Although their lips remained silent, their eyes spoke volumes. Every glance exchanged between them was filled with affection, understanding, and an unspoken connection that needed no words. They reveled in the simple joy of being in each other's presence, relishing the shared moments of silence and serenity. The car was moving on the roads, their hands were searching for each other's once again, they had just met and were hesitant whether to hold hands or not.

Priya stopped the car close to the theatre and stepped out of it, a gentle breeze rustled their hair, carrying with it the scent of anticipation. She had a playful smile on her face as she looked at him and said, "Do you often come to this place?"

He met her eyes and said, "I like movies but don't get the chance to come here often, free time is a rare luxury nowadays."

They both knew that their lives were filled with responsibilities and demands, leaving a little room to indulge in entertainment. But, in the moment standing outside the theatre, they formed an unspoken bond.

They took a walk, their hands entangled; they chose their words carefully as to maintain the tranquil ambience that surrounded them. as they walked on the street a charming restaurant came into view, both of them exchanged knowing looks and decided to step inside and grab a bite.

Stepping through the restaurant's entrance, a wave of aromas enveloped them, a waiter welcomed them and offered them a table. The cosy ambiance embraced them. the waiter gave them a menu and told them about their special combo offer on a Mexican burger. Priya decided to order the same.

"Could I have one Mexican burger, please?" she said.

Ajay looked at her and said, "You can order whatever you want," he said

The waiter patiently waited for Ajay to decide what to order as he was still looking at the menu.

Finally, Ajay looked up, "I'll have the Mexican burger, please," he said

The waiter noted down their order and said, "Your meal would be here soon, I appreciate your patience."

Both of them settled down in their seats eagerly awaiting their Mexican burgers, the aroma of freshly prepared food enveloped the air, making it a bit harder to wait for their food. Soon, the waiter came with two plates of Mexican burgers.

The waiter offered a genuine smile as he placed the plates on the table, The burgers looked amazing with colourful toppings accompanied by tasty golden fries.

Their mouths watered in anticipation as they prepared to indulge in the flavours that awaited them. they reached for their respective burgers, as they took their first bites, a symphony of tastes exploded on their mouths.

They sat there for a while after finishing their meal. Making the most out of their time together.

"Well, Priya," Ajay said, "what do you do?"

"I have done my MA, Ajay," she admitted softly. "I've applied to many places, attended interviews, but don't seem to have found the right opportunity yet."

"You've done your part, Priya. You have your MA, and that's a significant achievement. Remember that finding the right job is a journey, and sometimes it takes time. But it doesn't mean you won't get there."

"You're right, Ajay," she said, her voice full of determination. "I will not give up. I will keep finding new ways and keep finding. Maybe something unexpected will come my way, and it will be better than I could have ever imagined. But now there is a feeling of fear in my heart. After marriage, I will be left to become a housewife."

Ajay reached across the table and placed his hand gently on top of Priya's. "I'm not sure what our future holds, but if we get married, I will fully support your decision to pursue a career.

Priya's smile widened, a glimmer of hope rekindling in her eyes. She appreciated Ajay's unwavering support and his belief in her capabilities.

They made the payment for their meal, and stepped out feeling content for the entire experience.

As they were walking towards their car, Priya suggested, "Hey, maybe we should go to the famous Indroda park of Gandhinagar." Her voice had a spark of excitement.

"But by the time we reach the park, it might be late," he said

Priya was sad as she wanted to explore the park but she couldn't.

Ajay's heart compelled him to find a way to alleviate her feelings. "Listen, I have an idea. What if we head to the mall for some shopping?"

Priya's eyes sparkled as she heard that, her sadness was interrupted by the sudden surprise. An innocent smile emerged on her face.

"That's a great idea," she said, the promise of going for some shopping in the mall brought along a newfound excitement and an opportunity to make some memories in their shared journey.

They walked towards the car; their hands entangled embracing the moment to the fullest. Although they met each other for the first time in their life – it seemed as if destiny had already waved a collection of events that led to the moment they were experiencing.

They navigated the traffic on the way to the mall and parked their car in the parking lot. As they stepped inside, the chilly ambience of the mall enveloped them, as they started exploring the clothing section. While trying out some clothes, Ajay noticed a familiar face and knew it was Rocky. It's been a while since they met each other. He rushed towards him and pat him on the back.

"Hey Rocky." He said

"Ajay! What a pleasant surprise," Rocky replied, extending his hand for a firm handshake.

Priya observed the heartfelt reunion of two old friends.

Ajay turned towards her and said, "Priya, meet Rocky. He's been my best friend since we were kids."

"It's a pleasure to meet you," said Rocky extending a hand for a handshake.

"Likewise." Priya smiled as she shook hands with Rocky.

"It's been quite a while since we met, back in the days we used to meet on weekends usually at the bar and share our stories," said Rocky

"Those were golden days of our lives weren't they." Ajay said as he smiled

"Yeah, Those were the days." Rocky said, He felt a sense of nostalgia, but it didn't take him long to return to the present moment and grasp the reality of their busy lives."

"Hey, how about we go to a nearby cafe and get a drink? Just like the good old days!" said Rocky

"That sounds fantastic," Ajay said

Priya nodded in agreement, "Well it's good to see that you guys finally met." Her smile had a hint of gratitude for the moment. "I'd love to join you both."

With that decision they made their way out of the mall and headed to the café, as they entered the ambience of the café, the sound of cheers and clicking of glass was setting the mood for an evening of cherished memories.

Seated at a cosy table, they continued their conversation, they started sharing moments and soon their laughter filled the atmosphere. The bar tender served them drinks.

Rocky raised his glass, "Here's to old friends, new beginnings, and the beauty of life for bringing us together once again," Rocky said.

They clinked their glasses; the sound added more excitement to the moment they were savouring. Three souls entwined in the stories of friendship and life creating a perfect evening that they would cherish forever. As the evening progressed Ajay talked about how their fathers decided upon their marriage and they how they decided to stick around for a few days to get to know each other better before arriving at the conclusion.

"That's great, so how's everything going so far? Have you decided anything about the future?" Rocky asked.

"We have cultivated a good bond even though we just met today; we want to give ourselves time so the bond between us gets the time and space to blossom. But with her by my side I can say for sure that I can live a fulfilling life," Ajay said as he smiled at her.

Their eyes met, and they were getting closer to each other, somehow Rocky interrupted the intimate moment, "Okay guys, its late and I should get going, you guys can spend some more time over here if you like." A little gratefulness in his eyes could be seen at the moment for the beautiful evening he just spent with his best friend.

"We should get going as well; it's late, and your parents might be worried about you," Ajay said.

Sure, thank you for the amazing evening," She said

They left the café holding hands and stepped into the car, After a short drive, they reached Priya's apartment. he stopped the car in the parking area. it was obvious that they hadn't known each other for a long time but still somehow, they crossed each other's paths. Priya came close to him as she held his hand, "I'm grateful that we met." She said with a smile on her face, "I will always remember the time I spent with you."

He looked in her eyes and their lips met, for a moment it seemed like the time had decided to take a pause so the two souls can experience the moment to the fullest extent.

"See you later," he said.

Priya went upstairs and stepped inside her home. a splash of water on the face was enough to freshen her up. After having her dinner, she was sitting on her bed and checking notifications on her phone, as she didn't get the time to use her phone throughout the day.

She saw a bunch of notifications of missed video calls from her sister.

Priya had two sisters younger than her, living in Canada, youngest one was Anjali, she used to call her each evening and talk for an hour but that day was different, Priya was so immersed in living what she called the best moments of her life that she forgot to check her phone – that's something we're all aiming for.

Few minutes later she received a video call, and she immediately answered it.

"Hey sis! it's so good to see you!" Anjali said.

"Hey there, how's everything going?" Priya said.

"All good, what about you?" Anjali said.

"I had the best day of my life; you know what I met someone today and I just felt like there's something between us unarticulated," Priya said.

"Tell me more! I'm curious!" Anjali said.

Priya's excitement was at peak when she animated the story of how she met Ajay at a cosy café, their encounter turned into a delightful conversation that left each other yearning to spend more time and nurture the experience they were sharing together.

"And you won't believe what happened next," Priya said, "while we were strolling through the mall, we unexpectedly ran into Ajay's childhood friend Rocky. It was such a nice surprise, the three of us spent a wonderful evening at a café, laughing, sharing stories and cherishing memories. "

Anjali listened to her silently as the entire story unfolded Infront of her. "I like Rocky's name, and I'd like to meet him someday." Anjali laughed

"Anjali, will you stop this nonsense," Shreya interjected, "Hey Priya Didi, hope you had an amazing day, I loved listening about it." She was the second sister of Priya.

Priya's voice brimmed with excitement and anticipation as she shared the news with her sister. "You know what? Dad has made a decision. After our marriage, we are moving to Canada! Can you believe it?"

Her sister's eyes widened with surprise.

"That's incredible news! I can only imagine the adventure that awaits you!" Anjali said

"Exactly! It's like a whole new chapter of our lives," Priya said.

Their conversation continued, the distance between them seeming to shrink as they shared stories, laughter, and a sense of sisterly warmth.

Priya was feeling a bit tired and needed some rest, she disconnected the call and went to sleep.

The next morning, Priya's father opened the door, only to notice that Priya was still sleeping.

"Hey, Priya," he whispered "Time to wake up, my dear."

"Good morning, Dad."

"I have something wonderful to share with you. This morning, Ajay's father called me. He expressed that Ajay said "YES" for marriage."

Priya's eyes widened with a mix of surprise and joy. "Really, Dad? Ajay said yes?"

Her father nodded, "Yes, my dear. Ajay is eager to embark on this beautiful journey of love, it's a moment of celebration, you're about to step into a new chapter of your life. We'll soon start preparing for your engagement."

Priya's heart swelled with happiness as she absorbed the significance of the moment. She quickly hugged her father.

"Get ready my dear, your breakfast is ready." He said

Priya quicky went to the bathroom to freshen up and then she had her breakfast. She noticed a WhatsApp message from Ajay, he quickly opened it. It read "I knew you'd say Yes!"

A smiled emerged on her face as she read that "Of course, I would" she wrote. she knew that she was stepping into the new beginnings of her life, a single message evoked a blend of positive emotions in her, unveiling his deep understanding and love for her. what made her happy was that Ajay already knew what she would say before she even said that.

Meanwhile, Priya's father already started planning about the engagement, as Priya finished her breakfast, she noticed him writing in his diary about all the preparations.

He looked up with a warm smile, removed his glasses and invited Priya to sit next to him, He looked at her and said, "I've already had a conversation with Ajay's parents, your engagement, my dear, will take place in just two days."

Priya's eyes widened in surprise and delight. The next two days of her life seemed both close and yet too far away. Her heart was overflowing with joy and happiness.

"I've noted down the necessary arrangements and tasks that need to be completed. We have so much to do, but I am confident that everything will come together beautifully for this wonderful occasion."

"Dad, I can't express how grateful I am for your efforts." She said

"That's the little I can do for you, my dear."

As Priya and her father jumped right into the engagement planning, excitement filled the air. They set out on an extensive list of tasks and arrangements.

They needed to find the ideal location for the ring ceremony first. To make sure that the event would be memorable and enchanting, Priya's father worked tirelessly through the options, carefully taking into account every aspect. They finally decided on a stunning hall that radiated elegance and charm.

They focused on the guest list after securing the venue. Priya and her father reached out to their family members and joyfully announced the news of engagement. they ensured that every aspect of the event was carefully planned. They contacted caterers and selected a delicious menu for the occasion.

They were filled with anticipation as the engagement day drew near. The hall was prepared and elegantly decorated. The guest list was finalized, promising the presence of loved ones who would witness the beautiful occasion. With pride and affection in his eyes, Priya's father turned to face his daughter, knowing that their efforts had resulted in something genuinely lovely.

Although, she had been busy for two days, she still managed to stay in touch with Ajay, they would share stories of the engagement preparation over the phone calls as it was a once in a lifetime experience.

Later that evening Priya called her sisters to let them know about the wedding as they couldn't manage to attend the engagement. Both those sisters were in Canada and it was not possible that they could come.

Priya, feeling a mix of excitement and nervousness, clutched her pillow tightly in her arms. It had become her go-to comfort item, a source of solace during times of happiness and uncertainty. With her heart pounding in her chest, she reached for her phone and dialled Ajay's number.

"Hey, Ajay!" Priya said, her voice filled with anticipation.

"I can't believe tomorrow is our engagement day!" Priya said her excitement could be felt in her voice.

"Yeah, it's amazing right? We are getting engaged tomorrow." he said

"I've been looking forward to this day for a while now and its finally here." Priya said

" I too have been waiting for this day. Anyway, please let your parents know that they don't have to worry about anything, we'll make sure everything unfolds perfectly." Ajay said

"You've brought so much happiness in my life ajay, I'm forever grateful for that." Priya said

"I feel the same way, and I promise I will be there for you every step of the way. It's going to be a magical celebration of our love." Ajay said

She clutched her pillow even tighter, feeling a rush of affection for the man she was about to spend the rest of her life with. I'm so grateful to have you in my life. Tomorrow is going to be the beginning of an incredible chapter, and I can't wait to embark on this journey with you. Priya held her pillow close; she couldn't contain her happiness. The affection they felt for each other was like a flower blooming in its own miraculous way. she felt that her dreams were about to come true.

The long-awaited engagement day for Priya and Ajay had arrived. The morning sun illuminated the way for a new chapter in their lives. excitement filled the air. The meticulous decorations turned the location into a magnificent venue that radiated joy and celebration.

Priya, adorned in an exquisite traditional outfit, she felt a delightful mix of nervousness and anticipation as she looked at herself in the mirror. Meanwhile, Ajay, dressed handsomely in Indo-Western outfit, stood in the designated area, eagerly awaiting the moment that would bind their lives together. As they were going to weave these moments as stories on the fabric of their lifetime.

The engagement ceremony commenced, Priya and Ajay exchanged glances, their eyes speaking volumes of the love and devotion they shared.

The exchange of rings marked a significant milestone—an eternal promise of love, trust, and companionship. Applause erupted from the gathering, their family and friends showering them with heartfelt wishes and blessings. Amidst all the happiness brewing in the hall, she looked at him and soaked in the warmth of his presence.

The engagement day had become a memory etched in their hearts—a day that marked the beginning of a lifelong journey, woven in with love and shared joy of being together for each other – making promises that tranced the border of time.

Chapter – 2

With a gentle touch of the dawn, Priya slowly woke up, a soft smile tugging at the corners of her lips. The memories of the beautiful engagement ceremony from the previous day flooded her mind, bringing a surge of happiness that warmed her heart and soul. Sitting up in bed, Priya stretched and took a deep breath, feeling the warmth of the morning sunlight on her skin. She glanced at the wardrobe, contemplating on her outfit for the day. she wanted to choose something comfortable yet stylish.

After a few moments of thought, she picked a soft-colored outfit that perfectly complemented her. She stood in front of the mirror and stared at it for a moment. It reflected a confident and radiant woman.

Priya got ready, she stepped in her car and went straight to the theatre and waited for Ajay to arrive as he had already booked their movie tickets. she kept looking at the watch as each moment felt like an eternity. She wanted to call him and let him know that she was waiting but then she held back, perhaps waiting for someone has its own pleasure – it allows you the space to imagine different scenarios of how it would be like to meet them.

Few minutes later, Ajay arrived at the theatre. He took the parking ticket and parked his car at the parking area. He noticed that she was already waiting for him. A wave of joy washed over him. each step towards her, made his heart beat faster than usual. As he closed the distance, he could see her smile growing wider. He quicky hugged her, both of them didn't say anything for a while, savouring the joy of each other's warm embrace.

He held her hand as he broke the hug, and they went inside the hall, bought some popcorn and decided to take their seats as the movie was about to begin.

With the popcorn in hand, they found their seats – their fingers still intertwined. the lights began to dim, the screen started with a movie trailer the sound of which filled the atmosphere with excitement among the movie lovers.

As the movie began, they exchanged looks, leaned a bit closer towards each other, happiness bloomed within her. Soon they found themselves immersed in the captivating world of the movie. Each encounter deepened their connection, nurturing the bond they were sharing.

With the engagement celebrations still in the air, Priya's father started preparing for the marriage, he reached out to wedding planners, decorators, and caterers, ensuring that every aspect of the ceremony would be executed flawlessly.

At the same time, Priya and Ajay were making memories that they would cherish for the lifetime. They were too immersed in each other's company that they didn't realise the movie was about to end, the bright lights suddenly brought them back to the present moment.

The movie credits started rolling, they got up from their seats, hand in hand enveloped in the mixed emotions of happiness and love, the gentle breeze outside welcomed them as they felt warmed by the experience they just had.

They walked towards the parking area, with each step their connection bloomed savouring the joy of being together. As they reached their car, they felt feeling of reluctance as if they didn't want to leave. they shared a warm hug holding each other and delaying the fact that their time together came to an end for the moment. With a gentle touch, their lips met, sharing a soft kiss. It was a promise to each other that they would meet again soon.

They finally separated their lips and stepped back, they exchanged a good bye and stepped inside the car. as she was driving towards her home, memories of the time she spent flooded in her mind, making her feel both happy and sad at the same time.

Once home, she noticed a low battery notification on her phone, probably in the rush of the morning she forgot to charge it. She went to the bathroom and splashed water on her face which brought her a sense of relief, she gently wiped her face and went to her room. as she sat on her bed, she couldn't help but reminisce about the time she spent with him at the movie theatre. She could still feel his gentle touch on her lips and the warmth of his embrace, it all collectively evoked feeling of love and affection.

A notification on her phone broke the pattern of her thoughts, it was a message from Ajay, a rush of excitement rushed over her. With a curious anticipation she opened his message, "Dinner Tonight?" It read.

Unable to contain her excitement, she immediately typed her reply, "Absolutely! I would love to have dinner with you tonight" her words carrying a touch of enthusiasm and anticipation.

As she sent the message, she couldn't help but imagine the evening she would share with him, the stories and the memories they would create while she eagerly awaited the evening.

She put down her phone and started thinking about what to wear, where they would dine, and the endless possibilities that awaited them.

The remaining time seemed to slip away faster than she thought it would as she was eagerly waiting for the evening. She felt lost in a whirlwind of anticipation and excitement as she carefully picked up the perfect dress adding a touch of her favourite perfume.

As she was getting ready, she received a call from him, her heart skipped a beat when she saw his name flashing on the screen. She immediately answered the call, Ajay's warm voice greeted her, causing a surge of delight to wash over her.

"Hey, I wanted to let you know that I'm on my way to pick you up. I can't wait to see you tonight," he said.

"Really? That's wonderful! I'm almost ready," She said.

"See you soon! Take care," He said

"You too. Bye!" She said.

"Bye!"

They disconnected the call with an anticipation to see each other. While driving he couldn't help but think about her, how she would look like. Each moment made him crave her presence.

Ajay soon reached her apartment and parked his car in the parking area, his heart was beating faster as he went upstairs to her towards her home. She caught a glimpse of which from the window. A surge of excitement washed over her as she hurriedly made her way to the front door.

She quickly opened the door as he heard a knock on it. As she opened it, she was greeted with his warm smile, his eyes reflecting the joy of seeing her. They didn't need words – their eyes said It all.

"Hey Ajay!" Priya said.

"You look absolutely stunning tonight," Ajay said.

"Thank you, that's really sweet of you to say. Shall we head out?" Priya said.

"Absolutely! I can't wait for our evening together," He said.

Priya stepped out and locked the door behind her, with their hands entwined they made their way to the car downstairs. Ajay opened the door for her allowing her to step inside and then he closed the door. He sat on the driver seat and then they made their way to the restaurant. The drive to the restaurant was filled with easy conversation and laughter, the anticipation growing with each passing minute.

They reached the restaurant and parked the car in the parking area, as they stepped inside the restaurant, they were instantly embraced by the ambience, the soft lighting and soothing music playing in the background created a welcoming atmosphere.

A host greeted them and showed them a table, they settled into their chairs, taking in the intimate surroundings. Ajay gently took her hand in his, their fingers naturally entwining. His tender touch reaffirmed the love blooming between them.

A friendly waiter approached the table and handed over a menu, while suggesting their special dishes. After carefully selecting their dishes, they placed their orders. They shared a soft conversation on the table, stories of their life, dreams and aspirations – gradually unravelling layers of their personalities.

Their food arrived, and they eagerly indulged in the delicacies. savouring each bite with delight. Crating a beautiful memory – something they would continue to cherish throughout their lives.

The evening drew to a closure and they stepped out of the restaurant. As they went closer to the car, they found themselves enveloped in a moment of hesitation. Their eyes met – conveying the unspoken desire to extend the evening a bit further.

"I wish this evening could last forever," she said as she adjusted her hairs in the gentle breeze.

"I feel the same way, I don't want it to end either," he said

The two shared a brief silence, their hearts linked by an unspoken understanding. They were fully present, enjoying each passing moment as if time had momentarily stopped itself. The night stars were shining and on the other side, a romantic song was playing in the corner. Priya reached out, her fingers intertwining with Ajay's. Their hands fit together effortlessly, as if they were meant to be entwined forever. Their connection was deep, unbreakable, and filled with a profound sense of belonging.

They stood there for a while, cherishing the silence that enwrapped them. They reluctantly released each other's hands, knowing that they had to part ways for now and stepped inside the car. The journey towards Priya's home was filled with conversations of the evening, she told him how eagerly she was waiting for this evening.

And then they arrived at her apartment, he parked the car around the corner of the street which was almost empty as it was late in the night. The soft glow of the streetlight had already illuminated their path.

They stepped out of the car, he held her hand and said, "I don't want you to leave, could you please stay by my side forever?"

"I would love to, but this is where we part ways for tonight," she said. They kept looking at each other for a while. "I had an amazing time tonight, thank you for making it special."

He gently brushed a strand of hair behind her ear. "The pleasure was all mine," he whispered, making her crave his presence even more, "I'll continue to cherish every moment I spend with you."

They stood there for a while, silence filled the space between them, the connection they shared felt almost tangible weaving a thread of love each passing moment. Their lips came closer almost like an inch away from each other, the temptation for a kiss was real, gently their lips met and for a moment they felt like the time slowed down allowing their love to blossom.

"I should go," he finally said.

"See you soon," she said.

Ajay stepped inside the car and drove it away as she stepped inside the apartment gate with her heart filled with emotions and the memories they made.

After some time, Ajay's phone rang while he was driving. He stopped the car around a corner and answered the call.

"Hey my friend, how's it going?" Rocky asked.

"All good, what about you?" Ajay said.

"I was at the café, having a beer. Why don't you come over, will have a drink – just like old times," Rocky said.

"Sure, I'll be there soon," Ajay said.

Ajay too wanted a relief from all the emotions that clouded his mind. So, he decided to go to the café and have a drink. The journey towards the café was like an emotional ride – he couldn't help but think about her, she was the relief amidst all the chaos of life.

After reaching the café, he parked his car and went inside, only to notice that Rocky was waiting for him.

"Hey! Come over here my friend!" Rocky said. Excitement was clearly visible on his face, he seemed to enjoy his time at the café.

Ajay sitting next to him and said, "Hey buddy" His mind was still clouded by mixed emotions.

"What happened my friend, you seem a little off today?" Rocky asked.

"It's nothing." he looked at the bar tender and ordered a bottle of beer.

"You're missing her right?" Rocky asked

"I just dropped her home; we went for a dinner." Ajay said.

"That's something to be happy about, but it seems like something's bothering you." Rocky said.

"If I were to think about the wonderful things in my life for a moment, I would say that I just met someone who genuinely wants this relationship to flourish. She's willing to embrace the ups and downs of life with me," Ajay said.

"Go ahead, tell me more." Rocky said as he took a sip from the bottle.

"It's like I haven't told her about…" Ajay took a pause to collect his thoughts before saying a word.

"About what?" Rocky seemed curious to know more.

"I haven't told her about my past, the memories I made with her haven't faded. It's like I can't forget about everything that happened between us," Ajay said

"I assumed you already told her about your past relationships, since you two appeared to be more than just friends when she agreed to join us for drinks." Rocky said.

"I did, but not the details, I never told her that Anjali, her little sister was my girlfriend back in the days," Ajay said.

Just as he said that, he received a call from Priya, at first, he hesitated to answer it but he had to.

"Hi, I was missing you badly," Priya said.

"Hi, Miss you too!" Ajay said.

"You know what, I wanted to tell you about something. My sisters are coming to India tomorrow, as they couldn't attend our engagement," she said.

"That's great!" He wasn't sure about his words, as a sudden feeling of anxiety rushed over him.

"Are you okay?" She asked as if she noticed a sense of it in his voice.

"Yeah, I'm okay." Ajay said, trying to calm himself down.

"I just wanted to let you know that I'll be a little busy tomorrow because I need to pick them up from the airport. See you later than!" Priya said.

"Bye" he said and turned his attention to the bartender to ask for another bottle of beer.

He disconnected the call, but he couldn't disconnect himself from his own thoughts, he kept thinking about what would happen if she came to know about his past relationships.

The conversation at the café kept going, and he openly expressed whatever thoughts were troubling him, which made him feel better. As the night grew darker, he made the decision to head home. He bid farewell to Ajay with a handshake, saying, "See you later, my friend." He then got into his car and drove back to his home.

The next morning, Priya woke up a little earlier than usual, excitement filled the atmosphere in her home as her sisters are coming home after a long time. Her parents were tied up in the preparations – her mom cooked their favourite food while her dad went out in the market to buy some sweets.

Amid all the preparation for their arrival, she read a WhatsApp message from Shreya, "Hey Priya Didi, we'll be there soon" it read. They were apart from each other for years now, they had to meet virtually all this time, and finally her sisters were coming home. She jumped up from the couch, barely able to contain her excitement. She went back to tidying up everything around her and in the midst of that her mind wandered to the countless memories they had shared.

With each passing minute, her sisters' arrival felt closer. She couldn't help but imagine their shared laughter, the stories they'd share, the conversations and all. Once she was sure everything is perfect at the home, she took her car and drove to the airport.

While at the airport she eagerly waiter for her sisters, her heart raced with anticipation. Her eyes scanned the crowd, eagerly searching for familiar faces amidst the sea of strangers. And then, in the distance, she saw them – her sisters. A surge of joy washed over her, and she couldn't help but break into a wide smile. She felt her steps quicken as she made her way towards them.

Their reunion was a whirlwind of feelings, with lots of hugs, tears, and laughter. Years of separation vanished as they held each other close, acting as if they had never been apart. The overwhelming love and happiness that surrounded them made the airport seem to fade into the distance.

"I've missed you so much! It feels like forever since we last saw each other," Priya said.

Shreya eyes shining with tears of joy, replied, "I know, it's been too long! I couldn't wait to hug you again and feel your presence"

"This is like a dream come true," Anjali said.

"Absolutely!" Priya said. "The bond we have is irreplaceable."

"Tell me everything! How's life been treating you?" Shreya asked to Priya.

Their conversations turned to tales of their time apart as they made their way to the baggage claim area. They moved towards the exit carrying their luggage, Outside the airport, the busyness of the road, the noise reminded them about the good old days. Her sisters loaded their bags into the car, squeezing together in the backseat as laughter filled the air.

As they drove across the familiar streets around their home, smiles emerged on their faces, their smiles conveying a deep sense of contentment. The journey seemed to pass in an instant, as if time itself wanted to bring them back. After arriving at the apartment, they parked their car and went upstairs in their home.

When they entered through the front door, their mother was standing there with tears streaming from her eyes. Overwhelmed with emotion, she opened her arms wide, and the sisters rushed into her embrace.

"My girls, you're finally home. I've missed you more than words can articulate." her voice filled with love and relief.

Shreya voice choked with tears, "Mom, we've missed you too. It's so good to be back."

Anjali voice equally emotional, added, "We're sorry it took so long, but we're here now, and we're not going anywhere."

Priya and Anjali exchanged excited looks as Shreya dozed off peacefully, her fatigue from the long journey finally caught up with her. They hadn't had the opportunity to watch a movie together, just the two of them, in years. They sat down on the couch eager to make new memories and enjoy the simple pleasure of sisterly bonding over a movie.

While Anjali was immersed in the movie, Priya's thoughts drifted back to Ajay. she couldn't help but envision herself with him, watching a movie with their hands entwined. While she was lost in her thoughts the movie came to an end, they noticed it was evening already and Shreya was still asleep.

"Hey sleepyhead, wake up!" Anjali whispered in her ear. She slowly woke up and went to the bathroom to freshen up.

Meanwhile, Priya went to the kitchen and came back to the living room with some chilled beer bottles. She quietly placed the beers on the coffee table and settled back onto the couch, trying to contain her excitement.

Anjali turned her face to the table and noticed the beer bottles, "Did I miss something? What's the surprise?"

"No special occasion, just a little treat to make our evening a little more exciting." Priya said

"It's been too long since we had a chance to unwind like this."

Anjali's eyes sparkled with excitement as she reached for one of the bottles. "I couldn't agree more! Cheers to that!" she exclaimed, clinking her bottle against Priya's.

With their drinks in hand, they settled on the couch, their conversation flowing effortlessly as they caught up on each other's lives.

"Priya Didi, tell us more about Ajay," Shreya said

"Well, we met at the café, and then our conversations flowed, we were soon comfortable in each other's presence, later that evening we met his best friend and had a drink together. Each meeting seemed to nurture our bond – it seemed like we had known each other for years. And soon we got engaged," Priya said.

Shreya's eyes lit up with excitement as she took a sip from the beer bottle, "That's so exciting."

"Now it's your turn, tell us about how you met him," said Priya.

Shreya took a thoughtful sip of her beer, savouring the moment, before beginning, "Well, it all started on a sunny day, it was like an unexpected encounter which lead to a series of events and lots of ups and down, shaping the course of my life in ways I could never have imagined."

Her sisters leaned in closer, their curiosity was at the peak. As they eagerly awaited the details of how the events unfolded when she met him. Yet, amidst the anticipation, a crucial question kept yearning for the answer: Who was he?

Book 2: Chasing Memories

Chapter – 3

January 2017, Ahmedabad

It was one of those mornings when the time seemed to slip away faster than usual, Shreya couldn't afford to be late for the class again. She hurried through the bustling college campus; it was like a race against the clock.

Her sole focus was to attend the lecture on time, she intensified her movement, her heart racing with each step. As she rounded a corner, her foot caught on an uneven pavement, causing her to stumble forward. A stranger out – of nowhere held her arm, preventing her from falling.

Shreya looked up into a pair of mesmerizing eyes that held a sense of concern and amusement. He had a charming smile on his face.

"Are you alright?" he asked in his gentle voice blended with a sense of care.

Breathing a sigh of relief, Shreya managed to gather her composure and said, "Yeah, Thank you. That was close."

He looked at her for a moment, she looked pretty – an alluring soul.

He smiled. "Indeed, it was. You seem to be in quite a rush. Late for the class?"

Shreya nodded, "Unfortunately, yes. I've been struggling to manage my time lately."

"College life can get pretty hectic. Well, I hope you make it on time." He said

She bid him farewell and walked towards the class, she felt a sense of regret for leaving the encounter abruptly. Even though they didn't get much time to interact – he still left a lasting memory of their unexpected encounter.

She made it in time, she was grateful that she didn't miss out on her important lecture as she had to submit her assignment. As she settled into her seat, her mind couldn't help but replay the unexpected encounter.

Throughout the lecture, she found herself occasionally drifting off into daydreams, imagining future encounters with the same guy. There was an unshakeable feeling deep within her that their paths would cross again.

After the class concluded, Shreya and other students gathered their stuff and started leaving, Shreya packed her belongings and headed out of the lecture hall. She felt a sense of joy as she submitted her assignment which she worked really hard to complete before the deadline. She wondered through the campus hoping to catch a glimpse of him, but he was nowhere to be found.

Days turned into weeks and she didn't saw him again, she began to wonder if their encounter was nothing more than a fleeting moment that would fade away without even leaving a scent. She thought, maybe their paths were never meant to cross again.

She began living her life as usual, she immersed herself in her studies, spent time with her friends, and pursued her passions with unwavering dedication. She was often late for the class but that same encounter never unfolded.

She loved walking around the park, embracing the natural surroundings which allowed her to embrace the present moment. The vibrant hues of flowers blooming across the park and the gentle sound of the wind would often create a create a melody that soothe her soul.

After her lectures she would often go to the collage library, she would carry a few books with her, along with the academic ones. she loved to read. As if she found her peace in between the page folds. She found words for the emotions she was feeling – as if the author was somehow able to relate with her feelings and turn them into stories. She found her happiness in the silent ambience that books would often create around her.

She would often spend an hour or two in the library, because of which the librarian lady became her friend. The lady was a curious reader and would often suggest a few good books to Shreya. She enjoyed all types of books, whether they were fiction, nonfiction, occasionally thrillers, or old classics.

After the library hours, Shreya would make her way home, sometimes by bus and other times choosing an auto rickshaw. She would plug in her earphones and lose herself in her favourite music. Which made the journey towards home a little more entertaining. With closed eyes, Shreya would let the music guide her thoughts and emotions, allowing herself to be carried away by them.

She was never into relationships, in fact the only relationships she ever experienced were between the pages of the books. But then one day she saw him again.

It was a sunny Saturday; the college had organised a concert featuring her favourite band. The energy of the crowd was at its peak. the cheers and applause reverberated throughout the campus. As she immersed herself in the opening chords of her favourite song, she looked around at the crowd and then she saw him. He was standing nearby, singing along and lost in the music. She somehow summoned the courage to approach him and strike up a conversation.

She made her way through the crowd, heart racing with anticipation, until she stood next to him. With a radiant smile. "Isn't this concert absolutely incredible?"

"It's mind-blowing! I can't believe we have the same taste in music," he said.

As the music played on, they exchanged stories about their favourite songs, shared concert experience and discovered a myriad of common interests. The conversation flowed effortlessly as if they had known each other for much longer than just that moment.

"It seems you don't like to attend college more often," she asked with a playful smile.

"Oh, it's not like that, he laughed. In fact, I've been busy with some work lately and wasn't able to make it to the college regularly."

As the concert came to an end, they exchanged phone numbers, hoping to stay in touch. And then they walked towards the gate, as if they were trying to make the most out of their meeting.

"You added extra touch of magic to the concert with your presence," he said.

She couldn't help but laugh, "Is that so? What about you then? you seemed more energetic throughout the concert," she said, Trying to contain her laughter.

"Oh, I'm glad you noticed." He laughed with her.

As they were getting closer to the college gate, their steps slowed down, silence filled the distance between them. She tried to move her hand a bit closer towards him and he did the same. Their hands entwined for a while, and then he said, "See you later."

She nodded as she gently released his hand. She stood there for a while watching him walk away. "Even a brief meeting can leave a lasting impression on people," she thought.

Later that evening, Shreya found herself in her comforting home. Sitting in the cosy embrace of her room, she replayed their brief conversations, trying to grasp onto every word, every smile, and every glance they shared.

Her thoughts inevitably drifted back to him. The memories of their chance encounter, the fleeting moments they had shared, and the connection that bloomed between them. She found herself listening to the same songs that he liked, hoping she could find the piece of it that resonate with him. She wondered if he too thought of her if their encounter had left a lasting impression on him as it had on her.

The evening wore on, and as the world outside settled into a serene stillness, Shreya found herself lost in her own thoughts. she allowed herself to embrace the emotions he evoked in her.

The next morning after completing her lecture, she took her bag and walked out of the lecture hall and saw him. he was chatting along with his friends. She wanted to talk to him but wondering if it was the correct time for it. She decided to walk away pretending that she didn't see him.

He looked around in between the conversation and noticed her, he told his friends that he would meet them later and rushed towards her.

"Hey," he said as he was trying to catch his breath.

"Hi," she smiled. There was a natural ease between them as if they were old friends

"I couldn't help but notice you when you walked out of the lecture hall," he said. "Meeting you the other day left such an impression on me. I had to come and find you. I hope that's okay."

Her eyes sparkled with delight, " Yeah, it's okay, I've been thinking about that day too. I was wondering if we would meet again, and see, here we are!" her excitement was apparent in her voice.

A wave of relief washed over him, after noticing that she's been thinking about the same thing.

As they engaged in conversation, time seemed to stand still. They shared stories, laughter, and a genuine curiosity about each other's lives. The more they talked, the more they discovered common interests and shared passions.

In that moment, a new chapter unfolded, as if fate had already started weaving stories about them.

"Hey, would you like to grab a coffee someday?" he asked, as they were walking around the campus.

"Sure, that sounds like a nice idea," she said, "I believe I don't have any important lectures tomorrow, so tomorrow works for me."

That's great, I will wait for you at the coffee shop around 10 AM

"Fantastic! Let's meet at the coffee shop around 10 AM then," he said

It felt like time slipped away while they were immersed in each other's company. It was getting late, and yet they wanted to spend some more time together. He took her hand and held it gently; she seemed a little more comfortable with him. Their eyes locked for a moment, there was an unspoken understanding that connected them in some way.

"I wish I could pause the flow of time when I'm with you," he said

A smile emerged on her face, conveying her emotions.

"I feel the same way." She said

And then they parted way, each unexpected meeting was bringing them closer to each other. as if it was meant to happen. On her way home, she kept thinking about the coffee meeting, she started envisioning the scenario of them in the coffee shop.

After she was home, she had her lunch and went to her room, she was more than happy because of the bond she had cultivated with him – something that kept evolving. The shared memories, stories and every single meeting contributed to create an unspoken understanding between them that she had longed for.

She found her solace in thinking about him, she couldn't help but smile after knowing that they had truly cultivated a deep connection. She kept cherishing the moments they shared. amidst the chaotic world, he was her moment of peace.

Embracing the comfort of her home, she picked up a book from the shelf and started reading. It was one of those books that the librarian lady had gifted her. After reading a few words, she was able to resonate with those characters. As if she was vicariously living in the story, observing the characters as the story gradually unfolded. with each page turn she was delving deep into the characters.

Hours slipped by as she was immersed in her reading. She realised it was evening already. She felt like talking to him but wasn't sure if she should call him, but a feeling of hesitation gripped her. She took a deep breath and summoned the courage to make a call.

He picked it up instantly, she felt a bit of nervousness but she started the conversation.

"Hey, I was just wondering where we were meeting tomorrow," she asked.

"Well, how about that café nearby? The one close to the college," he said.

She smiled, "Sounds perfect. I can't wait to try their coffee."

As they continued talking, the familiarity of their conversation, the comfort in his voice, made her heart beat faster than usual, she couldn't hold back her true feelings any longer.

"You know", she said as she took a deep breath, "I miss being with you."

He paused for a moment before responding. "I miss being with you too"

"I cherish our memories each and every day," she said

There was a beautiful silence as if their unspoken emotions had filled the space between them.

"Can't wait to see you, to be with you" he said "let's make the most of our time tomorrow."

"Me too." In that moment, she knew that their bond was stronger than ever. There was a feeling of care and affection for each other, what they valued more than anything was each other's presence.

As they bid each other goodnight and disconnected the call, the moon light gently illuminated the room, she couldn't contain her excitement to meet him. there was a sense of tranquillity in the atmosphere, which allowed her to drift herself off in a peaceful sleep.

A picture of his smile was still vivid in her dreams, as if he was there in the room looking at her as she smiled at the thought of him.

The much-awaited morning had arrived, as the moon slowly disappeared behind the clouds. Morning rays gradually peaked through her window, casting a golden glow on her face. her eyes instantly opened and she woke up with contagious excitement, she couldn't wait to see him again.

She began preparing for the day ahead, carefully choosing her outfit for the day, each moment she spent getting ready was infused with the thought of him.

Time seemed to rush as she made her way to the café. Her each step took her closer to the moment she had been waiting for. Her heart was racing with the excitement, she kept envisioning him and her in the café, making the most out of their meeting.

Finally, she arrived at the café, she felt nervous but she wanted this experience to be a beautiful memory – something they'd continue to cherish throughout their life.

She stepped inside the café and quicky looked for a familiar face, then she noticed him standing alone at a table in the corner, lost in his own thoughts. she quickly made her way to the table and took a seat. A smile emerged on his face as their eyes met. everything seemed perfect in that moment, the cosy ambience of the café and the aroma of freshly brewed coffee added more magic to the scenario.

"Hey, good morning," he said, finally breaking the silence.

"Good morning," she said, still lost in his eyes.

"It's so good to see you," he said in a gentle voice.

"Good to see you too," she said.

They remained silent for a while, as If they were looking for the perfect words to say it.

"You have a way of making me feel comfortable, it's a rare gift to have," she said.

"You think so?" He smiled.

They ordered two cups of coffee, their conversation was slowly flowing like a stream from a river, and then he took her hand and held it gently. He reached across the table and their fingers intwined, their hands fitting together like pieces of puzzle.

They sipped their coffees and exchanged stories, he gently caressed his finger on the back of her hand, his tender touch conveyed a sense of affection.

Time seemed to stand still as they sat there, their hands entwined, sharing thoughts and dreams. The café bustled around them, and yet, the two of them created a tranquil ambience around them.

I feel so happy when I'm around you, it's like you are my definition of happiness, I can't find any other way to define it. He said

"I'm glad we are happiest around each other; I want to sustain this feeling as long as I can," she said.

"I feel the same," he said as he leaned closer towards her, she seemed a bit comfortable with that.

"I want you to stay with me, as long as life endures," he said.

They leaned a bit closer, as if they could hear their heartbeats racing faster than ever, they were more comfortable with each other than ever before, seeming to be immersed in the moment. she leaned forward and then their lips met, for a fraction of a moment everything seemed perfect. Their lips parted ways and he slowly brushed a thread of hair behind her.

He knew that they'd been at the café for a while and the time to bid farewell was closer than ever, but he wanted to express what he felt about her.

He gently leaned towards her and said, "I know it seems like we met a while ago and the way things have unfolded before us wasn't something we already planned for. but still what I feel about you is something genuine – I don't have the words to clearly articulate the same but I know you've already felt it."

She found herself completely enveloped in his presence. The warmth of his touch and the taste of coffee evoked a sense of charm. With their hands intwined they continued the conversation.

"I wanted to say this when we met at the concert, but I felt it might be too soon, but now we have the perfect moment to express our feelings." He caressed her hand gently, looked into her eyes and said "I love you, Shreya"

She felt the same about him, it's been a while since she wanted to express it, since they met, she kept weaving themselves in every moment of her life, the time she spent with him felt too little. her heart whispered the unspoken words, creating a symphony of her love and affection. The smile on her face and the joy for the moment completely articulated everything. But then, the moment had arrived, her emotions swirled within her like a whirlwind.

She had imagined this moment countless times, playing it out in her mind like a cherished daydream.

"I love you too," she whispered, her voice carried the depth of her emotions, the simple words had their own meanings for the two of them, it enveloped the connection that blossomed between them.

He couldn't take his eyes off her, he could feel a cascade of emotions flowing in his heart. the café stood still as they expressed their love, allowing it to bloom in its own unique way.

March 2023, Ahmedabad

Priya and her sisters sat around the table; their empty beer bottles a testament to the good times they had shared. As they savoured the last sips of their drinks, a subtle shift in the atmosphere caught their attention, The sky grew darker with each passing moment.

"Shreya, I must say, you have an incredible gift for captivating people with your storytelling," Priya said. She couldn't help but be completely enthralled as Shreya shared a narrative of her relationship in her collage days.

Shreya's words carried the weight of those emotions she felt about him. her sisters could capture the essence of their relationship.

"Thank you, Priya! I'm glad you enjoyed it! Collage days were truly special, I still cherish those days and the memories I made," Shreya said

"Absolutely! Your storytelling brought everything back to life, it felt like we were reliving those moments with you." Priya said.

Anjali said, "It felt like we were reading some kind of a novel."

"Shreya, You definitely have a gift for it," Priya said.

"Thank you, it means a lot to me. Those were the golden days of my life, something you only experience once in a lifetime," Shreya said.

They continued their conversation, laughter and warmth filled the air, intertwining their stories and strengthening their bond.

Meanwhile, Rocky was on his way home when he received a call from Ajay, he parked his car in a corner of the street and answered his call.

"Hey, meet me at the café. There's something I need to tell you," Ajay's voice had a hint of unease.

"Of course, I'll head there right away," Rocky said, swiftly getting into his car and driving towards the café. During his drive, Rocky couldn't help but wonder about the possible issue that was bothering Ajay. His mind raced with various scenarios, trying to piece together the puzzle of what could be troubling his friend.

He reached the café, parked his car and stepped inside. he immediately spotted Ajay sitting at a table, drinking a beer. Rocky approached the table with a mix of curiosity and concern, ready to hear what Ajay had to say.

"Hey Ajay, you wanted to talk? Is everything alright?" Rocky asked

"Hey, yes I wanted to talk to you about something," Ajay said

Rocky noticed that something was off, but not sure what. The least he knew, Ajay and Priya were preparing for their marriage, "There are so many things to be happy about. Something's bothering him for sure," he thought.

"Is everything alright?"

"I don't know, Rocky. Things haven't been going well lately."

"I understand Ajay, I'm here for you. What's been going on? You seem a bit different," Rocky said.

"Maybe, I should tell her about everything," he seemed a little worried.

"Tell her about what?" Rocky asked wondering what Ajay was talking about.

"I should tell her about my past relationships. I don't know if it would ruin the current one as well." Ajay asked for one more bottle of beer to the bar tender.

"It's possible that it would, but you shouldn't keep holding onto these things anymore. You have a great partner, don't you? She loves you, right?"

"I know," Ajay said. "I can't help but wonder if her sister were to reveal everything."

"I'm not sure about that, but What if she has already moved on with her life," Rocky said

"Do you really think so?" Ajay asked

"Of course, eventually people find ways to move on in their life," Rocky said

Ajay finished his drink; he seemed a little calm. Rocky's words gave him another perspective on life. Rocky also suggested the idea of buying a gift for Priya's sisters as a heartfelt gesture to show his affection towards her. Their conversation continued with the stories of their daily life; they laughed a little. As if they found comfort around the café, a place that allowed them to relive their pour their heart in the conversations.

Chapter – 4

On a bustling Sunday, Rocky and Ajay found themselves standing outside a crowded gift shop to buy gifts for Priya's sisters. The store was really busy but they somehow managed to find their way through the aisles and select some of the best gifts. They thoughtfully considered their choices and ultimately made their purchase.

"I'm glad we finally got the gifts. I hope Priya's sisters will like them." Ajay said Breathing a sigh of relief.

"Yeah, We put a lot of thought into choosing them. I think they'll appreciate the gesture." Rocky said

"Definitely. It's the little things that count, right?" Ajay said

"Absolutely. Now, let's wrap them up nicely." Rocky said

They approached the shopkeeper and requested for the gifts to be wrapped up. As they waited, Ajay's phone rang, indicating an incoming call from Priya. Ajay answered the call.

"Hey, Priya!" Ajay said

"Hey Ajay! Just wanted to let you know that me and Anjali are planning to go to the mall for some shopping. Do you guys want to join us?" Priya said.

"Absolutely! See you in a bit." Ajay said.

"Great, will wait for you at the entrance," Priya said.

They disconnected the call.

"It's the perfect opportunity, bro. You should give them the gifts right away," Rocky encouraged him.

"Couldn't agree more, let's hope for the best!" Ajay said.

They swiftly entered the car and made their way towards the mall. As they arrived, Ajay and Rocky noticed that Priya and her sisters were already waiting for them near the entrance. Priya's face lit up as she spotted them.

Ajay stopped the car close to them and they stepped out of it, Rocky was carrying a bag which had those gifts they recently purchased. Ajay's heart skipped a beat as he saw her.

Ajay was in a relationship with Anjali. It has been years since they last saw each other, their life had taken different paths since they decided to break up. Her memories hadn't faded, her presence brought them back to the surface. his heart was beating faster, as if he was frozen for a moment, lost in his own thoughts. Priya's voice seemed to have blurred away as she kept calling his name, slowly he came back to the present moment.

"Ajay, Are you okay?" Priya asked.

"Yeah, I'm fine," Ajay said.

"What happened to you? you seem a little lost," She seemed a bit worried about him

"I was actually overwhelmed by your presence; your beauty is truly mesmerizing," Ajay said.

Priya breathing a sigh of relief! She grabbed his hand, leaned a bit closer and whispered in his ear, "Could you please put that on hold for now? She said and let go of his hand.

"Anyways, I'm so glad you are here with us! Meet my sister Anjali."

"It's wonderful to meet you," Ajay said.

Rocky give a soft smile and said, "It's a pleasure to finally meet you in person."

They extended their hands for a handshake, and then they continued their conversation.

"We're excited to spend the day together. And what's in those bags? Are those gifts for us?" Anjali asked.

"Absolutely!" Ajay gave her the bag.

"That's so thoughtful of you! You really didn't have to, but I truly appreciate it," Anjali said.

"It's our pleasure. We hope you like them," Ajay said.

"Priya, I thought both your sisters would be here, but I can't see Shreya anywhere, is she here?" Ajay asked as he looked at Priya.

"She stayed at home to help my mom with some household stuff," Priya said.

"That's fine," Ajay said he seemed a bit calm after hearing those words.

After a brief conversation they stepped inside the mall. Rocky couldn't help but notice a hint of hesitation in Ajay's demeanour. Sensing his friend's unease, he offered a reassuring gesture, silently communicating that everything was going well so far.

They stepped inside the mall and started exploring different sections, In the midst of their exploration, Ajay and Rocky managed to find a moment to converse.

"I don't feel right, should we leave?" Ajay said.

"We've just arrived, and everything seems fine so far. Are you okay?" Rocky said.

"Yeah, I'm alright, but I think we could meet them some other time, right? I'd rather not be present when her sister reveals everything," Ajay said with a hint of worry in his voice.

"If that's how you feel, then fine. But, how would you convince Priya? Have you thought about that?" Rocky asked

"Maybe we can come up with some kind of an excuse?" Ajay said.

Rocky seemed lost in thoughts for a moment.

"Look, I understand how you feel right now, but you'll have to face this situation. even if you don't tell Priya about this, she would eventually find out. but as far as I know, I feel Anjali has really moved on in her life. And that's the reason why she hasn't told anything about her relationship with you, what if she doesn't want to ruin the one you have right now?" Rocky said.

Rocky's words always carried different perspective about situations, Ajay was really grateful to find a friend like him. Ajay understood what Rocky was trying to say. Maybe she has moved on, he thought to himself, also if I were to leave right now Priya would be upset about it.

He decided to stay, it was a hard choice to make but he did.

They continued shopping and exploring different sections of the mall, Priya bought a few cloths for herself, each time she would try something new – she would ask Ajay, does it look good on me? which brought a sense of happiness amidst the chaos of emotions. She thought about him in every choice of her life.

As the evening drew closer, they decided to head home, with heavy shopping bags. Everyone was rushing towards the exit, while Priya and Ajay slowed down their steps, trying to envelop themselves in the fleeting experience of the mall. They held their hands, their eyes locked for a moment trying to convey the stories of their own. They seemed to be completely immersed in their own world.

"The time flies so quickly when I'm with you." Priya said.

"I know, right? It feels like we just stepped into the mall, and now we're leaving. . I guess being lost in our own world makes everything else fade away." Ajay said, he squeezed her hand gently

"Isn't it amazing, sometimes our eyes find a way to say it all even if we don't find the words in the moment." Priya said

"True, it feels like our eyes have their own ways to tell what we're feeling." Ajay said

"You make me believe in the miracles of life. something beyond the words." Priya said

"For me, you're the miracle of life," Ajay said

She smiled, and gradually released his hand as the exit was closer than before.

"Oh, come on, guys! You're taking forever." Rocky laughed, He was waiting at the exit door along with Priya's sisters.

"Don't worry, Rocky, We won't keep you waiting for long," Priya smiled as they stepped out of the mall.

They looked at each other for a while, as if they didn't want each other to leave. Time seemed to stand still as they locked their eyes. it was an end of a long and amazing day. he slowly reached for her hand, intertwining their fingers.

"See you later than!" Ajay said.

"Sure, see you later!" Priya said.

He released her hand, and slowly walked away their eyes remained locked until they reached for their car. Priya and Anjali decided to go home as it was getting late.

Rocky and Ajay decided to head over to the café to unwind and continue their conversation in a more relaxed setting. They left the mall behind, their shopping bags in hand, and made their way to their favourite café. As they stepped inside the café, the gentle jazz music in the background welcomed them, the cosy ambience of the café provided a much-needed relief from a long day at mall.

They found a quiet corner table and settled onto their seats; Ajay ordered two bottles of beer as he was sponsoring the drinks.

They continued their conversations, sharing funny stories from their shopping trip. Laughter echoed throughout the café as they recalled amusing encounters and surprising finds at the mall.

"I'm glad you decided to stay, making any excuse would eventually upset her." Rocky said

"I know right? That's the reason I chose to stay," Ajay said.

"Did you notice something? Anjali already moved on in her life," Rocky said.

"You are right, but I am worried about Priya. I don't want her to get hurt," Ajay said.

"Eventually she would come to know about all this, what if she were to ask you about your relationships before you move ahead with your marriage? Have you ever thought about that?" Rocky asked.

"I know that someday I will tell her about everything about my past relationships." Ajay said.

"Come to think of it, you haven't told me much about her either." Rocky said, He finished his bottle and ordered another.

"From the very first moment I saw her, she gave the impression of being a timeless beauty, captivating in every way. it's been years but I still remember those times when I was with her." Ajay said.

"Memories are really tricky you know, even the happiest ones can bring a cascade of tears in your eyes." Rocky said.

"Totally agree with that, it seems that the bar tender replaced the beer with something else, my friend has become a philosopher." Ajay laughed

"Might be a different brand than usual." Rocky laughed

Their laughter spread everywhere, filling every corner with an irresistible feeling of joy. There were cheerful conversations filling the warm and cosy atmosphere. People sat together at small tables, deeply engaged in lively talks.

As the night grew darker, they found themselves completely absorbed in the cosy ambiance of the café. It felt like they were savouring every moment, determined to make the most of their experience that day. The warm lighting and soft music enveloped them, creating a comforting atmosphere that made time seem to slow down.

"Anyways, tell me about how it all began." Rocky said

Ajay took a deep breath, "It all began on a rainy day, our paths collided in the most unexpected way. She decided to embrace the weather by taking a walk in the park, I somehow gathered the courage to strike up a conversation. That was the moment when it all began and everything fell into place In a way we never imagined."

July 2016, Ahmedabad

It was an enchanting morning; the rain had just stopped leaving behind a captivating atmosphere. There were still some water drops on some flowers around the park. The rhythmic sound of birds chirping amidst the rain-soaked park could be overheard, as if they too were indulged in the beauty of the morning.

Ajay walked briskly through the park, embracing the beauty of nature, he glanced around the park only to notice a beautiful girl walking slightly ahead of him, occasionally she took pictures of the flowers as the rain drops made them look even more elegant. She seemed to blend effortlessly with the beauty of nature. He was totally captivated by her presence.

Ajay quickened his steps, hoping to catch up with her. he was curious to strike up a conversation with her, he gradually went closer to her. he was drawn towards her smile as if she was truly grateful for the moment Infront of her.

"I must say, the park looks even more enchanting after the rain," Ajay said, his excitement was obvious.

She looked at him, with a sparkle in her eyes, "Absolutely! The rain always adds a touch of magic to everything."

"I couldn't help but notice how beautifully you blend with the park's surroundings. My name is Ajay, by the way."

"I'm Anjali. Thank you for your kind words."

They continued walking along the park amidst the tranquillity of nature, exchanging stories of their life and passions for the future. Ajay was moved by her deep connection with the world around her, her presence seemed to amplify the beauty around her. their conversation flowed effortlessly jumping from one topic to another. He later learned that her name was Anjali.

Our conversation has been truly captivating; would you be interested in continuing this wonderful exchange of words over a cup of coffee? Ajay asked

As they walked, he felt like there was a connection between them, something that worked like an inner compass, nudging them gently towards a common destination.

The café was nested close to the park they were in, they stepped inside the café, a delightful fragrance of freshly brewed coffee floated in the atmosphere, enchanting their senses.

The soothing ambience of the café was ideal for their connection to bloom. They immersed themselves in their conversations over the cup of coffee, with each moment, their connection grew deeper, like two streams merging in the same river.

Ajay took a sip from his coffee, "You know the coffee around here is incredible, but today it seems your presence has added extra touch of magic to it."

Anjali's eyes sparkled with delight, "Thank you, Ajay." She smiled.

Their conversation flowed seamlessly, filled with laughter, shared dreams, and heartfelt moments. The more they talked, the more they discovered the intricate layers of themselves.

Their cups emptied and they stepped out of the café, as they started walking on the streets, The sky had turned a gentle shade of grey, the wind carried a hint of upcoming rain.

"It seems the rain is inviting us to embrace its magic," Ajay said

"I think nature understands our emotions far better than people," Anjali said

"Couldn't agree more. By the way, should we continue our journey with raindrops as our companion?" Ajay asked

"Yes, I think it's going to rain soon, so we should hurry," Anjali said as she looked at the sky.

They started walking, dark clouds gathered overhead, casting a shadow upon them and soon the rain began kissing the earth. They continued walking, surrounded by the cascading raindrops, as if they somehow found solace in their melodic sound.

Their hands would occasionally collide with each other which began a reason to make an eye contact and exchange smiles, embracing the beauty of the rain.

While walking along the slippery road, her feet lost their grip for a moment, but he reached her and grasped her hand preventing her from falling. They exchanged glances, an unspoken understanding bloomed between them, he could sense that she felt comfortable in his presence. The rain seemed to add an extra layer of magic to the scenario. the scent of rain-soaked earth filled the air.

They found a shelter under a tree and stole a moment to converse amidst the captivating scenario. Their hands still entwined, as if they had their own stories, something that could only be felt by them.

"I'm glad we found a shelter." She said.

She would occasionally extend her hand to feel the touch of raindrops.

"The atmosphere seems even more beautiful when we are together." He squeezed her hand gently.

She looked into Ajay's eyes and said, "I feel the same way."

Loving someone is easy and complicated at the same time, easy as the night embraces the moon in a starry sky, complicated as looking for sunlight on a rainy day. She was the sunshine he longed for.

Drenched in each other's silence, the rain adorned their hairs and clothes, making them feel alive, allowing them to be fully present in the moment, as if the rain itself was painting its artwork on the canvas of life.

Soon, it stopped raining and left behind a beautiful atmosphere. she took a step forward from the shelter of the tree and looked up at the sky,

"The rain has stopped, isn't the atmosphere peaceful?" She said.

"It is, But I must say, walking in the rain with you had a certain enchantment to it," Ajay said. "As if the rain itself was bringing us together, revealing a deeper connection between us."

"I feel the same way." She smiled "there's something enchanting about sharing stories while walking on the rain-soaked streets."

"Yeah, sometimes a simple conversation becomes the most adventurous moment of our life, revealing parts of ourselves that we long forgot." Ajay said

"Honestly, walking with you and talking to you became an unforgettable memory, whenever I would revisit those moment, I would be able to feel the same feelings." Anjali said

"I can totally relate with you. I guess it's about time we should leave before it starts raining again." Ajay said

"If it does than we'll experience the same things again till the end of our journey." Anjali said as she smiled at him.

The rain had already stopped when they walked out of their shelter and continued their journey, The air felt fresh, the tranquil ambience enveloped them.

After approaching Anjali's apartment, she turned her face towards him,

"It was the most amazing day of my life; I really appreciate it." she said.

"The pleasure was all mine, I'm glad we got to share this special experience together," he said.

The sunset painted the sky with its vibrant hues, turning it into a mesmerising canvas. They stood there for a moment, reluctant to part their ways. They took out their phones and exchanged their numbers hoping to stay in touch. They found themselves in a moment of reflection, recollecting the memories they made throughout the day, their stories, their walk on the rain-soaked streets, all intertwined with the vibrant colours that painted the sky. It felt like it all happened in an instant. Everything ended up evoking a sense of gratitude for the day they just experienced.

The day light gradually faded, and then with a smile on their face, they parted ways.

April 2023, Ahmedabad

Ajay and Rocky were sitting in the café, their beer bottles were now empty after their conversation, Rocky listened to him silently as the highs and lows of Ajay's relationship unfolded before him. the air was thick with the emotions he poured in the story, it seemed like a river of memories flowing effortlessly, each word containing a blend of joy and compassion.

Ajay took a moment to collect his thoughts, a smile emerged on his face with a mix of gratitude and acceptance. "You know, Rocky, sharing that story felt like a weight lifted off my shoulders. It's been a long time."

"I can imagine, I'm glad you decided to open up and share." Rocky said

"Yeah, you know it's tough sometimes, I can't imagine what Priya would think of me when she learns about all this." Ajay said

"Just concentrate on your wedding preparations for the time being; we'll figure something out." Rocky Said

"Anyways, Thanks for listening the entire thing." Ajay said

"You don't have to thank me, that's what friends do right?" Rocky said as he placed his hand on Ajay's Sholder.

That evening some of the unwritten chapters of Ajay's life unfolded, carrying the moments he shared with her, each word containing the raw emotions he felt back then.

"It's getting late, I think we should head home." Rocky said as he looked at the watch.

"You're right, Rocky. It's been a wonderful evening." Ajay said

"Shall we gather our coats and settle the bill then?" Rocky stood up and stretched his body.

"Absolutely." Ajay said

And with their bill settled, they stepped out of the café, carrying with them the echoes of their conversations.

Meanwhile at Priya's house, the family gathered in the living room, talking about the marriage preparations. Priya's parents set on the couch, Priya, adorned in a traditional outfit, sat beside them, her eyes sparkling with a mixture of happiness and nervousness.

Priya's father Looked at his daughter with a smile and said, "Priya, your mom and I were planning for a family dinner at a fine restaurant."

Priya's face lit up with excitement, "That's great, it's been a while since we've all spent some time together."

Priya's mom joined the conversation, "Also, you should invite Ajay."

Priya blushed slightly and said, "Sure mom, I'll invite Ajay."

Anjali seemed excited about the plan, "When are we going?"

Priya looked at her mom and said, "How about tomorrow evening?"

Priya's father, Sure, the restaurant owner is a friend of mine," I'll call him and book a table for tomorrow evening."

They knew that this gathering for a dinner would create cherished memories, and extend their warmth for someone close to Priya's heart. They eagerly anticipated the laughter and joy that would fill the air as they shared this special occasion with Ajay.

As the night progressed, the sky grew darker lit up with the shining stars, they continued cherishing their memories.

But Priya seemed lost in thoughts, her mind drifted off to the thoughts of Ajay. Priya couldn't help but imagine what their meeting would feel like, Priya imagined small gestures, glances, and touches that would reveal the bond they shared. her imagination was so vivid that she could feel the warmth of his touch and the comfort of his presence.

Book 3: Shattered Promises

Chapter – 5

Priya's morning began with excitement, she couldn't wait for the evening to arrive so she could finally meet him. she has felt the same thing before, when he asked her for the dinner date. But things were different that day, she would have to keep her emotions in check as she would be accompanied by her family. But for her, even a look from him was enough to evoke a havoc of emotion.

She simply couldn't contain her excitement to see him at the restaurant, she counted hours, minutes and even seconds as she eagerly awaited the evening.

She went about her daily routine but her mind was preoccupied with the thoughts of Ajay, she could notice a smile emerging on her face each time she thought of him. each passing hour felt like an eternity. She would occasionally imagine how their evening would look like, replaying scenarios over and over.

The sun began to set as the evening approached, the moment she eagerly anticipated was here. She knew that each moment would lead her closer to him.

Priya nervously dialled Ajay's number.

"Hey, Priya!" Ajay said

"Hey, I simply wanted you to know that my family and I will be there at the restaurant soon." Priya said

"That's great, I'm on my way to the restaurant, can't wait to see you!" Ajay said

She felt a sense of happiness and comfort as she heard those words from him. she took a deep breath, trying to calm her racing heart. "I'm excited to see you too, it feels like an eternity has passed since we last met." Priya said

"I feel the same way! I'll be waiting for you at the restaurant!" Ajay said

"I can't wait to be with you!" She said.

They disconnected the call, a sense of joy washed over her; she couldn't contain her happiness.

Priya's family reached the restaurant, Priya's eyes lit up as she noticed that Ajay was already waiting at the door, they quickly approached him and greeted him.

After some formal greetings they stepped inside leaving a moment for Priya and Ajay to converse.

He slowly reached her hand, held it gently, and said, "You know, I've missed you!"

"Missed you too!" Priya said

In the midst of their conversation, they took a pause. She noticed that her family members have already stepped inside. Ajay looked at her, she felt her heart racing as she tried to make an eye contact. He leaned forward, as their fingers entwined. she felt an unspoken invitation, as if an unspoken desire was brewing beneath the surface. Priya's heart raced as she leaned in ever so slightly. Their faced drew closer, the space between them narrowed gradually.

Their lips met, sharing a gentle kiss. in an instant their lips parted, knowing that they'd have to step inside the restaurant. It was the most beautiful fleeting moment they had ever shared. It felt like they left an imprint of their love and affection on each other's lips, something that won't ever fade away.

He slowly released her hand and they stepped inside, only to notice that her family was already waiting for them to arrive. Ajay and Priya approached the table.

"Ajay you're finally here! Please have a seat." Priya's father Said as he looked at Priya and Ajay, noticing their evolving bond had filled his heart with a sense of joy.

"Ajay, were so glad you could make it." Priya's mother said.

"Of course! How could I miss such an amazing evening!" Ajay said, there was a sense of nervousness in his voice.

"So, Ajay, how has work been treating you lately? Priya's father asked.

Ajay's nerves eased as he engaged in a discussion with Priya's family.

"Work has indeed been demanding with the new project, but I'm passionate about it and determined to make it a success." Ajay said

"Priya, I can't see Shreya anywhere, isn't she joining us?" Ajay Asked as he looked at Priya.

Hearing this, Anjali looked at Ajay and smiled, "Actually, she had some work to do, so she's staying at home."

During dinner, Priya's family expressed their joy by recounting stories of Priya's pranks as a child, reflecting on priceless memories. Ajay listened intently, showing a sincere interest in the stories narrated by her family.

Their meal drew to a closure, Ajay appreciated their efforts for making the evening memorable for a lifetime.

Priya's father raised his glass, "To Priya and Ajay, a couple filled with love, affection, and a bright future together!"

Happiness bloomed between Priya and Ajay as they felt the love and warmth from her family.

Priya's father settled the bill while other waited for him, a sense of contentment enveloped them. Ajay reached out his hand to help Priya up, their fingers interlocking once again.

As Priya and Ajay prepared to leave the restaurant, Priya's father turned to them with a warm smile.

"Priya, you guys can take your time. Don't worry about being late. Enjoy your evening together." Priya's father said.

"Thank you, Dad. We'll make the most of our time together," Priya said.

"Thank you so much, it means a lot to us," Ajay looked at Priya!

"Enjoy your evening, and remember, make memories." Priya's father said.

They stepped out of the restaurant, Ajay bid farewell to Priya's family hoping to catch up again. her family stepped inside the car and headed towards home.

Ajay looked at Priya, their hands fitting together conveying stories of their own.

"Ready to go?" Ajay asked

"More than ready, the evening's been incredible!" she said, her voice filled with excitement.

"This is just the beginning." He said

"Where should we go?" She asked

"Anywhere, just you and me." He smiled

They settled into the comfortable seats of the car, eager for a peaceful drive where they could enjoy each other's company and the scenic views along the way.

Leaving the restaurant behind and immersing themselves in the moment. they rolled down the windows, allowing in the gentle breeze. Ajay selected a romantic playlist, filling the car with melodies that perfectly complemented their drive.

They made their way to the riverfront, a place that held a significance for them, it was the first place they visited on the day they met. after reaching the riverfront, they parked their car and stepped out, their hearts brimming with anticipation and nostalgia.

They walked on the river front, hand in hand as the gentle wind carrying the echoes of the love they shared. The colourful reflections of the lights around the riverfront danced on the surface of the river. The sun was slowly fading behind the clouds, illuminating the river surface with the orange glow.

They found a spot, a bench overlooking at the river, they settled on it. Embracing the beauty of the river front. They looked into each other's eyes, their hears overflowing with love and gratitude. They started sharing stories of their first meeting, immersing into nostalgia, recalling the moments that cultivated the feeling of love.

As they sat there, enveloped by the peaceful atmosphere, they paused to soak in the beauty of the riverfront at night. Lost in the moment, they watched as the river gently flowed.

She looked at him a smile playing on her lips, "You know, Ajay, I feel grateful to have you in my life, I never imagined that our first meeting would end up leading us all the way until this very moment."

"Every day with you has been a blessing" he smiled at her, from the day we first met I knew there was something special about you."

Priya reached out and gently squeezed Ajay's hand, "I feel the same about you"

Ajay looked at the river and said, "We've made so many beautiful memories together."

The moonlight gradually illuminated their surroundings, Ajay leaned in closer, his heart brimming with affection. Their eyes locked, and in that moment, time seemed to stand still. With utmost tenderness, their lips met, sealing their connection with a gentle, passionate kiss. a silent promise of their unwavering devotion to one another.

"It has been such a wonderful day, Ajay. The drive, the riverfront, and our loving conversation. I feel so grateful for everything." She said

"I couldn't agree more, it was truly magical. Spending time with you and reminiscing about our journey together." He said

"Absolutely, I would love to remain in this moment forever. But, it's time to head home. I'm looking forward to simply being with you, for forever." She said

"I don't want this moment to end either, but I'm truly grateful to have you as my life partner." He said

"That's all I could ever ask for, Ajay. I can't wait to see what future the holds for us." She said

Ajay leaned in and kissed her on her cheek. "I love you, Priya, more than anything else in the world."

"I love you with all my heart." She said.

They stepped inside their car; their hearts filled with gratitude for a wonderful evening they shared, and headed towards home.

Their conversations faded into silence, as the wind continued to play with their hairs. Their minds drifted off to the moments of the evening, their walk on the river front, their conversation everything ended up deepening their relationship.

They soon reached Priya's apartment, they stepped out of the car, their eyes met. Ajay gently held her hand.

"I don't want this evening to end." He said

"Me neither." She Said

"We'll soon be together and won't have to endure the suffering of being apart." He said

"I can't wait till we would finally be together." She said

"I feel the same way, but for now we'll have to part ways," he said as He slowly released her hand.

"Bye, Ajay."

"Bye Priya."

Their eyes remained locked as they parted ways, Ajay stepped inside the car and drove off. While Priya stepped into her home, a familiar feeling welcomed her. as Priya quietly made her way through the hall, she noticed that the lights were dimmed and the atmosphere was tranquil as usual. she noticed that her parents were asleep

Priya splashed cold water on her face, allowing the refreshing droplets to awaken her senses. She couldn't help but smile at her reflection in the mirror. She put her phone on charging ignoring the countless notifications.

She approached Shreya quietly, as she was still awake watching a movie on her laptop.

"I see, you love watching movies." Priya said in a low voice trying not to disturb her family members who were asleep.

"Hi sis, how was your day?" Shreya said as she removed her headphones.

"Amazing, you know had the dinner at a restaurant and then Ajay and I went for a drive at the river front that place holds so much memories." Priya said

"That's great. And yeah, I love watching movies," Said Shreya.

"What makes you love them so much?" Priya asked.

"Actually, in movies everything seems perfect, including the lives of the characters," Shreya said.

"You do know that the lives of these characters are curated and not real." Priya said

"I do, I can't ignore the fact that the stories leave an imprint on your life. They change you in some way," Shreya said

"Is that so? Why don't you tell me a story? Something that left an imprint on your life." Priya said

Shreya took a deep breath, "One day, in the midst of the city's vibrant energy, two souls collided unexpectedly, completely unaware of the journey that awaits them. their encounter forever changed the course of their lives. each meeting seemed to bring them closer to each other."

Priya interrupted her, "hold on, could you please mention the name as well, it sounds interesting." Her smile reflecting her curiosity.

"I'll let you know at the end of the story," Shreya said

"Yeah sure, please continue." Priya said

"It all began in the month of March 2019, when fate was weaving threads, setting in motion a love story that transcended time itself."

"Collage brought them together unexpectedly, their encounter evolved into a blossoming friendship that soon became an inseparable bond. their heart found solace in each other's presence, a companion they could resonate their emotions with and a love that transcended their wildest dreams. But their story was far from perfect, they were both flawed individuals with their own insecurities and past wounds, something that often overshadowed their hearts, at some point they noticed that everything between them was gradually falling apart."

She continued narrating the story and Priya listened silently immersing herself in it like a character of some kind, what she didn't know was that Shreya wasn't narrating a story from a movie, but rather from her own life.

August 2018, Ahmedabad

It was a cloudy Saturday, he sat inside his car, patiently waiting for Shreya outside the college gate. He wanted to spend some time with her. He glanced at his watch, realizing that Shreya's classes were just about to end. As the final bell rang, signaling the end of the class, he spotted Shreya walking towards the college gate. With a smile on his face, he parked his car nearby and reached for his phone. He dialed Shreya's number and waited for her to pick up.

"Hey, Shreya. I'm here, Waiting for you at the gate." He said

Shreya's cheerful voice came through the phone, "That's great! I'll be there in a minute!"

He put his phone aside and took a moment to think about her. Shreya was the light of his life, and he cherished every moment they spent together. He leaned back in his seat, looking around, eagerly waiting for her. His eyes lit up as he saw Shreya approaching the gate. She had a radiant smile on her face, and her eyes sparkled with excitement. He quickly stepped out of the car as he couldn't wait to meet her.

Shreya wrapped her arms around her, returning the affectionate gesture. "Hey, handsome! Thank you for picking me up. It seems you finally got some free time for me."

"I'm really sorry about that, but today is all about you, my dear." He said

She laughed as she heard that. "So where are we going?"

"Anywhere you wish to go." He said

"Let's go to my favourite bookshop," she said. "I really want to get some new novels, and then we can figure out where to go next."

They settled inside the car and drove to her favourite book store, after navigating the traffic of the busy Saturday, they finally reached the book store.

They stepped inside the cosy book store and began to wander through the aisles, running their fingers along the spines of various books. enveloped in the magical world of books surrounding them, they engaged in small conversation, she talked about her favourite books, authors and genres while he listened to her silently.

"You know, books are filled with stories, wanting to be read by someone." She said

"That's one of the reasons why you love novels, right?" He said

She smiled as he said that, their hands naturally found each other's, fingers weaving together, articulating their affection.

"I love being here" she said

"And I love being here with you," He smiled at her. "In your presence it feels like book has come alive." He said

"You always know how to make me feel special." She said

"Because you are my special person." He said

Their fingers remain entwined as they walked through the book store, occasionally exchanging glances at each other. she picked up her novels and they stepped out of the book store.

"Want to go for the lunch somewhere?" He asked

"Sure, but where?"

"I'll take you to my favourite place." he said

Her eyes lit up with anticipation, eager to experience the delights that had won his heart. They made their way to the restaurant, exchanging light-hearted conversation along the journey.

In the cosy ambience of the restaurant, they enjoyed not just the tasty food, but also the special moments they shared. Their connection grew stronger as they relished their favourite dishes.

"I'm so glad I could bring you to my favourite place." He said

"It's incredible. I can tell why it holds a special place in your heart. Thank you for sharing this experience with me." She said

"You deserve the best, my dear." He said

"I'm so happy to have you by my side." She said

"Being with you is what I call happiness." He squeezed her hand gently.

Later that evening they found themselves walking along the park, trying to embrace their time together to the fullest extent.

You know Shreya, "I really enjoy spending time with you." He said

"I feel the same way, I often dream about meeting you." she said

"I'm not complaining; I'm just expressing how I feel that sometimes we fail to prioritise this relationship." He said

"I know how you feel, but there's something I wanted to talk about." she said

"Please, go ahead." He said

"You know I really love you and I want to be with you. I've given this a lot of thought, but..." she couldn't find the right words to say it.

"What?" A hint of worry in his voice.

She took a deep breath before continuing, "I've decided to go abroad and continue my studies further, my sister has been helping me prepare for the same."

"You know we won't be able to meet for years, right?" he said

"I know it won't be easy." She said trying to calm herself down.

"But what about us? Can our relationship survive the distance?" He said as his eyes gradually filled with tears.

A havoc of emotions surged within her, as if she wanted to pour everything but she couldn't find the exact words to put it, eventually her eyes said it all, unable to contain the overwhelming emotions, a cascade of tears rolled through her eyes. she held his hand gently hoping to convey what words couldn't.

"You know, life wasn't as happy and vibrant before I fell in love with you, without your presence there won't be anyone around to infuse colour on the canvas of my life." He said as he wiped his tears.

He dropped her home, during the journey both of them remained enveloped in silence, the weight of their unspoken words ended up distancing them even further.

Days turned into weeks, unseen messages and unanswered calls piled up. eventually the conflict that arose from the silence became a barrier separating them emotionally. as if the bond they cultivated became a fragile thread ready to break at any moment. Each passing day added another layer of distance between them. Deep within their hearts there was a faint hope that they would meet again, as if they yearned for each other's presence but not finding the words to speak up.

One day their paths collided at the same place they first met, Priya was walking along with a professor gathering information about studying abroad, when she saw him.

Their eyes locked for a moment; she took her leave from the professor. He went closer to her. both of them remained silent – lost in their own thoughts. and finally, he broke the silence.

"Hi, Shreya." he said

"Hi, Ajay." she said

"Can we talk? I mean if you're free than…" He said

"Yeah sure." She took a deep breath.

"Look Shreya, I know it's your dream to go abroad, but have you ever given a thought about how it would affect our relationship? You know that we won't be able to maintain it like we used to." He said

"I know how you feel, but I have made up my mind. I know it's not an easy decision for me to take, but we might consider moving on from this relationship." She choked as she said that.

"I'll never forget the times we spent together." He said

The tears in their eyes blurred things away for a moment. He held her hand for one last time, drew her closer and hugged her.

"Good bye Shreya, maybe one day our paths will collide and we'll wonder about how everything fell apart." He said

"Good bye." She said as a cascade of tears rolled through her eyes.

And then they parted ways, with their heavy hearts and teary eyes, at the same place where they first met, a series of events happened and they bloomed a beautiful relationship. Their hands reluctantly slipping from each other like an ephemeral moment disappearing in the fabric of time. They waked away keeping the memories as fragments of their love.

April 2023, Ahmedabad

Shreya took a deep breath before completing the story she was narrating to Priya who had been listening to her silently, trying to comprehend each part of the story. "And that's how everything was falling apart. the relationship they once cherished, became a memory fading away into the sands of time"

"It's tough to imagine what they must have felt, I can feel their pain." Priya said

"I know, it's like they became strangers in the very relationship they cherished." Shreya said

"It breaks my heart to think about how they handled those feelings." Priya said

"Relationships are like petals of flowers, they can be beautiful when we put in the effort to cultivate them, but they can be fragile at the same time as one little touch can break them apart." Shreya said

"I couldn't agree more." Priya said

"Anyway, it's late. You should go and sleep." Shreya said she turned off her laptop and went to her bed.

"Sure, let's get some rest. Good night, Shreya!" Priya said

The silence in the room allowed Priya to reflect on the events of the story that unfolded before her.

Life can be unfair at times, sometimes you have to choose between what you want now and what you want the most — sometimes both feels important. In Shreya's life staying in the relationship was important as she had cherished every moment she spent with him, it first started as a fleeting encounter, later on became a relationship that they nurtured with their love. but it ended up creating an emotional void in their life.

Priya decided to take some rest and she went to sleep in her room. she lay in bed enveloped by the darkness of her room, the moonlight spreading across the sky. she closed her eyes her thoughts started to wander. she found herself standing in some familiar street, at first, she wasn't able to grasp what the way but later on she noticed a few familiar things in it, she had a feeling like she's been here before, some faint sounds kept reverberating in her mind, she looked up at the sky, dark hues of stormy clouds stretched across the horizon, the temperature dropped slightly, wind carrying a hint of rain as it whispered through the trees, in the midst of that rain was only a matter of time. she extended her hand to feel the gentle touch of rain drops. As she looked around, she saw a couple completely drenched in the rain, absorbed in the love of the moment, but she couldn't see their faces, as only their silhouettes were visible. later she noticed they were getting closer, their voices were slightly audible. Their faces slightly visible but she couldn't guess who they were, and then her vision was suddenly interrupted by the thunder strike right before her, in the panic of the moment she quickly covered her eyes with her hands — as she couldn't witness what just happened, she gradually removed her hands from her eyes only to notice the couple was gone, she rubbed her eyes but no luck. Her heart was racing faster than ever. Unable to contain the tension of the moment, she quickly woke up from her bed, trying to catch her breath.

She looked around the room, her eyes gradually adjusting to the familiar surroundings. She turned on the night lamp and the soft golden glow illuminated the room.

She set up in bad wrapping her arms around herself, as if she was trying to seek some comfort, she took a deep breath and exhaled slowly, anchoring the thought that it was just a dream.

Chapter – 6

Shreya's friends, learned that she was staying in India for her sister's marriage, and made a plan to meet up. they organised a party at a resort and asked Shreya to join them, although Shreya initially rejected but as her friends kept insisting, And then she agreed to join the party.

Later that evening, she stood Infront of the mirror, adorned in her favourite dress, ready to transition into party mode, her reflection in the mirror radiated confidence and excitement for the evening ahead. With a final glance at her reflection, Shreya flashed a satisfied smile. Taking a deep breath, she walked out of her house and settled in the car.

"Shreya, you look absolutely stunning in that dress!" Priya said

"Thank you, Priya Didi! I'm beyond excited for tonight," Shreya said

"You're going to be the centre of attention." Priya said

Shreya laughed as she heard that, "It's nothing like that, anyways, thank you for giving me a ride.

"No need to thank me." Priya smiled.

She soon dropped her at the resort, Enjoy your evening! She said.

"Yeah sure." Shreya said.

As she made her way through the crowd, the resort seemed to come alive with the music and a sea of vibrant outfits. Her friends welcomed her to the party and admired her stunning appearance.

She seamlessly transitioned into the party mode, letting the music guide her movements. Her friends brought a tray filled with drinks to make things even more exciting

The party came alive with the colorful lights and the energy of the people enjoying every bit of it. She couldn't resist her friends as they offered her a variety of drinks to try out, each one promising a unique blend of flavors, Shreya reached for one of the drinks, its vibrant hues reflecting in her eyes. With a quick swirl, she brought the glass to her lips, savoring the first sip.

As she continued to indulge in the drinks, she began to feel the effects of them. The room around her started to spin, she struggled to maintain her balance, her vision gradually blurring, making it harder for her to navigate through the crowd. Her friends noticed that something was wrong, They approached her, offering a helping hand and guided her to a quieter corner of the resort.

After the party was over Shreya's friend called Priya, letting her know about the situation.

"Hello, Priya..."

"Hey? Is everything okay?"

"Actually, Shreya is slightly drunk because we were partying."

"I'm really sorry about that, please look after her." Priya was really worried about the situation, as it never happened before.

Priya quickly called Ajay and informed him about the situation, Priya had to stay home and maintain lowkey, as her parents would worry about her if she panicked about the situation.

Ajay was sleeping, enjoying the tranquility of his dreams, when his phone abruptly rang. He stirred, his eyes still closed, instinctively reaching out to answer the call. He could feel the urgency in her voice. Priya went ahead and explained the entire scenario, Ajay's heart raced with concern. Without a second thought, he quickly stood up from his bed after hanging up the phone, his mind already racing, as he hurriedly made his way to the bathroom.

Ajay splashed cold water on her face to wake himself up. He put on a T-shirt, went out, and sat in the car.

After an hour-long drive, Ajay finally arrived at the resort. As he stepped out of his car, He scanned the surroundings, searching for Shreya amidst the crowd. His heart was beating faster than ever as he saw her in group with of her friends.

Ajay made his way towards the group. he felt a sense of relief as he saw that Shreya was alright. Trying to contain his emotions, he spoke with a hint of relief and concern in his voice, "Hey, Shreya! I'm so glad you're fine. I just spoke to Priya, and she told me about this, so I'm here to pick you up."

Shreya remained silent, trying to avoid an eye contact. once they reached the car, Ajay helped Shreya to sit on the passenger seat and closed the door. He took a deep breath, trying to focus on prioritizing her safety above all else. As they drove away from resort, Shreya broke her silence.

"Why the fuck did you come here, after all this time." Shreya Said

"What are you saying Shreya?" his voice filled with concern

Shreya's eyes narrowed, her anger intensifying. She leaned back in her seat, crossing her arms defensively. " Who asked you to come and pick me up?" she asked, her tone dripping with fury.

"Priya told me to pick you up." he said, trying to concentrate on driving while talking to her.

Ajay gripped the steering wheel tightly as he felt his heart racing in his chest.

"Stop the car, Ajay!" Shreya said

Ajay pulled the car over to the side of the road; his heart was racing faster than ever. Shreya's words took him by surprise.

"Why did we fall in love, Ajay?" Shreya said. tears welled up in her eyes.

Words eluded him as he found himself lost in his thoughts.

"I know how you feel, it was difficult for me to forget everything we once shared. But we both decided to move on, didn't we? he said.

She wiped her tears as she contemplated on his words. she looked into his eyes, looking for the same comfort she felt years ago, "I don't want to let go of the love we shared, but the pain of remembering is overwhelming."

Ajay offered her a water bottle. She sipped some water before saying anything.

"It's like you cross your paths with someone, you forge an emotional bond only to be controlled by the circumstances that shatter everything away. All that remains are haunting memories. " She said

Gently, he reached out and wiped away her tears, his touch filled with tenderness. "We both deserve happiness, and Nothing would make me happier than to see you smile again."

After making sure she was okay, he started driving, both of them didn't say a word, lost in their own thoughts, their minds replayed the events from their past, the memories they made together, a simple unexpected encounter bloomed into a relationship and then gradually like the petals of flowers everything fell apart.

Ajay noticed that Shreya had fallen asleep, he realized she needed rest and solace. Carefully moving through the streets, Ajay navigated his way to Shreya's home. He glanced at her as she was sleeping peacefully, his heart filled with a mixture of affection and sadness.

Ajay carefully parked the car and turned off the engine as they approached her apartment. He noticed that Priya was already waiting for them to arrive.

She quickly approached him as he stepped out of the car and hugged him.

"I'm really grateful to have you in my life Ajay." Said Priya

"I feel the same way." Said Ajay

He unbuckled Shreya's seatbelt and whispered softly, "Shreya, we're at your home."

Shreya woke up slowly, feeling a bit disoriented. Her eyes fluttered open, and she glanced around, feeling momentarily confused about her surroundings. But soon enough, she recognized where she was.

Priya gently held Ajay's hand, her touch filled with trust and love. "I know I can always count on you, Ajay," she whispered

Ajay smiled reassuringly, his eyes meeting hers. "And I'm always there for you, Priya"

In that shared moment, their eyes locked, reflecting the depth of their connection. As if they found a moment of comfort just by looking at each other.

Shreya, still in a slightly intoxicated state, "Hey, you guys, you're testing my patience!"

Her light-hearted remark brought a smile to everyone's faces, Priya, catching her breath from the laughter, turned to Ajay and said, "Well, I should head to my home now. Goodnight, Ajay." She gave him a warm smile before leaving.

Ajay looked at her, "Sure Priya. Goodnight."

He too was grateful for her presence in his life, He couldn't help but feel a sense of longing and contentment as she disappeared from view, knowing that they would see each other again soon.

Ajay settled in his car, he began to reflect upon the events of the evening, he knew that Shreya still had feelings for him. Deep down, he understood that she needed someone to help heal the emotional wounds she carried. He was aware that he could not minimise her suffering, regardless of the fact that they had taken different paths, their connection still remains — of course it's not the same as before.

Ajay stopped the car on the side of a quiet road and stood by it for a while, he felt the weight of the worries that clouded his mind. He had been trying to reach out to Rocky but he wasn't responding to his calls. Rocky was the only person who could help him to cope with these feelings. It felt like the fate had decided to unfold situations against his favor. With each passing moment his heart was beating faster, he made up some of the worst-case scenarios in his mind. Amidst all that he relied on smoking to get an instant relief from his thoughts.

While the weight of the situation overwhelmed him, he was distracted by the sudden sound of his ringtone. He took his phone and saw Rocky's name flashing on the screen. Relief washed over him as he instantly picked up the call.

"Hey Rocky, thank goodness you called back," Ajay exclaimed, his voice slightly shaky. "I'm in a tight spot, and I need your help. It's about Shreya..."

"What happened?" Rocky asked

Ajay took a moment before saying anything, "Can we meet? Let's talk about this in person."

"Yeah, I'll see you in a bit and then we'll talk about it. I'm on my way to Sindhu Bhavan Road, lets meet over there."

"Sure, I'll be there soon." Ajay said

Ajay settled in his car and drove towards Sindhu Bhavan Road, after reaching there he waited for rocky to arrive. After waiting for a while, Rocky arrived at meeting the place. He swiftly parked his bike on the side of the road, his mind focused on the task at hand.

"Ajay, what's going on?" Rocky said, "Tell me everything."

"It's been a whirlwind, Rocky," Ajay sighed, his voice heavy with emotion. "Where do I even begin?" He paused for a moment to gather his thoughts, trying to find the right words to describe the chaos he was feeling.

"You remember Shreya, right? we were in a relationship back in the days, but then she went to Canada and we broke up. Unfortunately, we met today. All those emotions, the memories, the love we shared still haunts me. I thought I had moved on but I still haven't healed those emotional wounds."

"I get it but, isn't she Priya's younger sister?" Rocky said.

They remained silent for a while, as if he was wondering what to say, he felt the whirlwind of emotions inside him.

"Come to think of it, you haven't told me anything about it." Rocky said

"It's a long story buddy, maybe some other time." Ajay said

Rocky broke the silence, "I understand what you might feel about all this." Rocky said, his words filled with empathy, hoping to offer some solace amidst the chaos.

Really?" Ajay said, his voice laced with frustration. "Do you understand the magnitude of this mess I'm in? Both Shreya and Anjali are my ex-girlfriends. Can you imagine the complications and the fear that grips me, what would happen when Priya would learn about all this?"

Silence settled between them once again, but this time it was filled with a shared determination to confront the situation head-on.

"Take your time to process those emotions, my friend; it's your personal journey. remember that life is constantly evolving, happiness is waiting for you just around the corner." Said Rocky

"You're right; in order to fully embrace the present, I must first learn to accept the past as a part of my life and then gradually let it go. I know that Priya needs me more than anything else."

As they stood there, he could feel the weight of his emotions for her, as if someone had opened an old wound. But he knew that he had a friend to give him a different perspective on each and every situation of his life. the path ahead might be difficult but he would get through it somehow.

Their conversations continued to flow as they caught up on their everyday life, Ajay talked about his marriage preparations and the dreams he has for Priya. He wants her to experience the best of her life.

Meanwhile, Priya turned off the night lamp and fell sleep, her mind wondered into a vivid landscape, the place seemed familiar, she found herself in a captivating scene.

Amidst the heavy rain, a couple walked the street, drenched from head to toe. Their hands were entwined, the raindrops syncing with their heartbeats, as if nature itself created a mesmerising melody. Each step they took was accompanied by the rhythm of the rain.

Their eyes had stories of their own, conveying everything in a silent language of love and affection, The raindrops adorned their entangled hands like delicate jewels.

Rain continued to cascade around them, with a tender touch, they closed the gap between them, their lips meeting in a soft and passionate kiss. The passing seconds became insignificant as they surrendered to the moment's sweetness. with the tender touch of their lips, In the wonder of witnessing the ethereal scenario the ,world seemed to held its breath.

Priya stood there trying to comprehend things, a sudden blow of wind caused her to close her eyes for an instant, and then as she gradually opened her eyes the couple disappeared. Priya instantly woke up, realising it was a dream – just like before.

Priya turned on the lamp, and drank some water from the bottle, she tried to calm herself down. But her heart continued to race, refusing to be pacified. The dream haunted her thoughts, its vivid images refusing to fade. Who were they, that strange couple that seemed entirely foreign and yet deeply familiar?

Book 4: Embracing Dreams

Chapter – 7

As the morning light approached, Ajay and Priya were busy with the final stages of their wedding preparations. The air buzzed with excitement and anticipation as their special day approached. Ajay couldn't help but feel overwhelming joy and happiness as he knew it would soon be together.

In the midst of bustling wedding preparations, Ajay took a moment to pause and soak in the beauty of their journey. The trials they had overcome, the unspoken sacrifices, and the unwavering belief in their love had led them to this point of profound joy.

The thought of waking up next to Priya every morning and embarking on the journey of a lifetime filled Ajay's heart with warmth and anticipation. he imagined their future together, a home filled with love, sharing dreams and endless possibilities.

Lost in his thoughts about their future together, Ajay's daydreaming was abruptly interrupted by a phone call, it was Priya.

"Hi, Ajay." she said a bit hesitation in her voice

"Hi, Priya." he said

"I was wondering if you're free right now. Can we meet?" Her voice carried a hint of unease as she spoke

"Of course, Priya. You sound a little different today. Is everything okay?"

Priya remained silent for a moment, she took a deep breath and said, "Yeah, I'm fine. Let's meet at the café."

"Sure, I'll head over there. See you soon." He knew that something was bothering her for sure.

Ajay felt a wave of curiosity and a bit of worry as he hung up the phone. He wondered about what Priya might be going through, he soon made his way to the café.

Ajay stepped inside the café, looking around the café, only to notice that Priya was sitting in a cosy corner eagerly waiting for him to arrive. a warm smile emerged on her face as he approached her.

"Hey, Priya," he greeted her warmly.

"Hey, she said

Are you sure everything's okay? Ajay asked sensing a bit of unease in her voice.

Ajay, "she began, "I wanted to talk to you about something. I had a bad dream."

Ajay leaned in closer, giving her a bit of comfort.

"Tell me about your dream Priya." he said.

Priya took a moment to gather her thoughts before describing the details of her dream, "In the dream, I saw a couple completely drenched in the rain. They were standing together, lost in their own world. But then, suddenly, there was a flash of lightning, and at that moment, I closed my eyes. When I opened them again, the couple was gone, and then I woke up, my heart was beating faster, I took a sip from my water bottle to calm myself down."

He reached out and gently took Priya's hand, offering comfort. "That sounds intense, Priya. Are you okay right now?"

"Yeah, I'm okay but you know what there's a feeling of uneasiness that won't fade away."

"I understand what you're saying Priya, it's completely okay, just realise it was a dream." He gently held her hand.

"But there's something else I wanted to tell you, that couple I saw in my dream - although their faces weren't clearly visible but still, they seemed so familiar."

He gently caressed her hand, "Dreams can be mysterious sometimes, and may evoke feelings of uneasiness, but please know that you're safe with me."

Priya put her head on his shoulders as if she found comfort reflecting on his words. "Thank you, Ajay. for being with me and listening to me," she whispered.

"Of course, Priya, You can always count on me. I'm here to support you through everything," Ajay said.

In that moment, a comforting sense of understanding enveloped them both, strengthening the bond they shared.

Meanwhile, Ajay kept wondering why the scenario she described sounded so familiar. The dream she described — a couple walking along, drenched in the rain, there was something about it that resonated with him.

Lost in thoughts, Ajay tried to recall similar incidents happened in the past, memories teased him with bringing some fragments of his past on the surface. He tried to explore the depths of his memories to unravel the forgotten fragments of his past, hoping to uncover the origin of this familiarity.

And then suddenly like a flash of insight, a faint image came his mind, The scenario Priya had described in her dream mirrored a significant moment from his own past.

Ajay decided to keep the connection between Priya's dream and his previous relationship a secret. He thought about the possible consequences of telling the truth and got caught up in a whirlwind of emotions.

Ajay became overwhelmed with conflicting emotions as they sat in the café. On the one hand. He desired openness and transparency in their relationship. On the other hand, he feared that revealing his past could hurt their blossoming relationship by causing feelings of insecurity and uncertainty.

Ajay made the difficult decision to keep quiet, at least for the time being. He wished to keep Priya from any needless suffering or confusion that the revelation could bring.

Ajay noticed a worried look on Priya's face, he took a deep breath to collect his thoughts, "Priya, I appreciate the fact that you decided to open up about your bad dream. Sometimes dreams can hold deeper meaning that we may not fully understand."

Priya leaned forward as her interest grew. "Ajay, do you believe this dream might have some meaning? It felt so real, and I have an uneasy feeling that there may be more to it."

Ajay hesitated for a moment, wondering whether to revel the connection from his past or keep it to himself, finally he chose to speak. "Priya, your dream deeply resonated with me, evoking memories from my past. But I'm not sure if it holds complete relevance."

"Please tell me more about it, Ajay," Priya looked at him with a sense of concern.

He took her hand in his as he gently reached across the table, "Priya, the scenario you shared, relates with a moment from my past relationship. But please know that my feelings for you are real, I cannot change my past but I can embrace my present."

Priya's eyes widen with a mix of surprise and wonder, she squeezed his hand gently, silently urging him to continue.

"Priya, I want you to know that you mean the world to me, I have carried that experience with me but it's in the past. You are the one I've chosen wholeheartedly, the one I want to build a future with."

"Thank Ajay, for trusting me enough to share this. I want us to embrace our present, lets create our own story far beyond the shadows the past." Priya said

"Let's cherish the love we have; I want our present and future to be filled with joy and happiness. We can forge a beautiful past ahead, leaving behind the ghost of the past." Ajay Said

Ajay navigated their conversation to lighter topics as it went on, making Priya feel loved, supported, and cherished. After spending quality time together, Ajay and Priya reluctantly realized that it was time to part ways for the moment.

"I had a wonderful time Ajay, thank you for sharing your thoughts with me, I am grateful to have you in my life." Priya Said

Ajay looked at Priya as they stood at the door of the café, "The feeling is mutual, Priya. You bring so much joy and love into my life. I can't wait to see you again soon."

"No matter where life takes you, please know that my love is forever by your side." Priya said

They held each other's hands for a moment, savouring the connection they shared. They parted with a final smile, carrying the warmth of their shared moments in their hearts, and walked in different directions. The anticipation of their next meeting fuelled their spirits. they knew that their love would only grow stronger during their time apart.

Ajay stepped inside his room; his mind consumed by thoughts of Priya's dream.

He couldn't help but feel a strong urge to delve deeper into his own memories, He wanted to untangle the threads of the dream that Priya shared.

he tried to dive deep into the past, trying to find the sunken fragments that hadn't faded. And then suddenly everything was back on the surface again. He found himself lost in a whirlwind of emotions, vividly recalling moments from his past relationship. Each memory became a puzzle piece.

As he sifted through the memories, The rain-soaked couple and the feeling of being torn apart — it all danced before his eyes merging with his own memories.

He recalled the taste of rain on his lips, the strings of her hairs soaked in the raindrops, the intimate moment he shared under the darkened sky, it all intwined evoking a havoc of emotions.

Ajay's heart skipped a beat as he connected the dots, He recalled those moments – walking in the rain with their hands entwined, the shared silence that enveloped them, the slightly audible rhythm of the raindrops, it all came back to the surface again. he saw the clear resemblance between Priya's dream and the moments he shared with his past love – Anjali and Shreya.

September 2016, Ahmedabad

It was a rainy day, and the sky was filled with dark clouds. but Ajay and Anjali decided to go out and embrace the beautiful atmosphere. They explored the rain-soaked streets of the city. The raindrops cascaded down, creating a soothing melody as they tapped against the street.

They noticed how the rain had altered their surroundings as they walked. The streetlights' gentle brightness was softly reflected by the trees' leaves, which were sparkling with raindrops.

They soon stumbled upon a sanctuary, nestled amidst the chaos of the bustling city. A stone pathway led them through a dense forest, where raindrops sparkled on the leaves. the air containing the scent of the flowers, refreshing their senses with each breath.

"This place is magical, just like you" Ajay gently swiped a stray raindrop from Anjali's face with his hand.

"Everything is magical in your presence, my love." She said

Ajay took her hand in his, their fingers intertwining like a perfect fit. "Every moment spent with you feels like a beautiful chapter in our love story."

Anjali leaned closer, her voice barely a whisper. "Ajay, I feel comfort and love in your embrace, which makes overcoming all of life's difficulties worthwhile."

"Being here with you feels like a dream." He whispered as he leaned closer

Their words became the melody that danced in the air, expressing the depth of their emotions and the strength of their connection.

"I want to create a future with you, Anjali, a future full of shared dreams, joy, and love." Ajay said, his voice laced with determination.

Anjali's heart filled with love and affection as she heard those words from him, as if she was living some kind of a dream. "I believe in us, Ajay. With you, I am ready to embrace the unknown and create a beautiful life." her voice filled with tenderness.

Spending time in the sanctuary was like a peaceful retreat from the noisy world, they found a space where their love can blossom.

As they were walking on the streets, completely drenched in the rain with hand in hand, Suddenly, a bright flash of lightning illuminated the dark sky, Anjali quickly embraced Ajay as she heard that. her body pressed against his,

Ajay smiled at her; he knew that she found comfort in his arms irrespective of the situation. He whispered gently, "you're safe with me Anjali"

Anjali's eyes sparkled with gratitude and trust. In that fleeting moment they felt the depth of their connection, their souls intertwining in a passionate embrace.

Their lips met in a gentle kiss, sealing their love amidst the thunder and rain. As if they stole an intimate moment amidst the melody of the raindrops.

Their lips parted, rain continued to cascade around them, Anjali's lips curved into a smile, "Thank you Ajay, for loving me so deeply."

"I've met a lot of people in my life, but none of them have ever had such a profound impact on me as you have." He said

"I feel the same way" she smiled

"You know, sometimes I feel like everything reminds me of you, the blooming of flowers, raindrops, sunset sky, moonlight – everything. As if you left fragments of your soul in them." he said

"It feels wonderful to know that I have such a special place in your thoughts." She said

The evening light gradually faded into the night sky, Ajay and Anjali knew it was the time to part ways, the rain ceased, leaving behind a captivating atmosphere.

They stood there, reluctant to let go of each other's hand. Their fingers interlaced beautifully as they savoured their final moments together.

"I wish we could stay in this moment forever," she whispered, her voice carrying their shared desire.

His eyes filled with both tenderness and a touch of sadness. "I know, Anjali. It feels like time moves too quickly when I'm with you. but remember, No matter where we are, we carry each other in our hearts."

"You're right, Ajay. Distance may separate us physically, but our love will always bind us together" she said

In that moment they made a silent promise to be there for each other. they reluctantly parted ways with the anticipation to meet again soon.

A gentle current of time carried Ajay and Anjali along its flow, revealing a subtle change in their relationship. They weren't spending enough time together anymore. They missed the special moments they used to share as busy schedules kept them apart. Time together felt different, lacking its warmth that they once shared.

The lack of emotional intimacy became more apparent, as Their conversations became shallow and lacked depth of love that once fuelled their relationship. Without the emotional connection their conversations became mere exchange of words.

They started missing each other's calls, taking longer to respond to messages, and cancelling plans more frequently than they had previously. The familiar feeling of understanding and acceptance slowly faded and was replaced by the growing distance.

Days turned into weeks and weeks turned into a month and then they finally decided to meet in the usual café, it was late in the evening, they sat across the table, sipping their drinks.

"Ajay, we used to be a great relationship. but it seems like we're gradually losing touch." Anjali said

"I know right? our lives have become extremely hectic. We seem to be running from one thing to the next, barely having time to breathe." Ajay said

The once effortless flow of their conversation now seemed forced, as if they were searching for topics to fill the gaps of silence.

Ajay couldn't help but feel a sense of sadness, he thought that the time apart would become a reason to reunite them but instead it seemed to increase the distance between them.

Anjali, too, was aware of the changes in their relationship. She found herself struggling to express her thoughts and emotions, as if a barrier had formed between them. the ease with which they once shared their words seemed to fade away between them.

They both longed for a sense of comfort and familiarity that they once found in each other's presence.

They finished their drinks, exchanged a few words, their smiles masking the underlying tension that had infiltrated their once vibrant relationship. And with heavy hearts, they agreed to part ways, hoping that some time apart would give them the space and perspective they needed to rediscover themselves.

They felt as if they had reached crossroad on the path of their life, their eyes met conveying a flood of memories and shared moments that seemed to stretch back through time.

The silence between them seemed to hold the weight of their unspoken words, as if their eyes already whispered the pain in their hearts In a final gesture of affection, they embraced each other, their touch had a sense of tenderness and farewell. They held each other for one last time, and their intimacy and connection was apparent. And then, they released each other gently, freeing themselves from the ties that had once bound them.

Deep down they knew they made a tough decision, their hearts still yearned for the love that gradually faded.

The sky remained clear and it didn't rain that day, as the raindrops could have unleashed a torrent of emotions between them.

Chapter – 8

May 2023, Ahmedabad

Ajay was at his home immersed in the memories, It felt like he had just returned from a long journey through time, exploring the depths of his past. he could feel the gravity of those moments as they brought back the old feelings.

He wiped his tears realising that the memories brought along a flood of emotions, as if they carefully preserved fragments of his past.

In that moment it felt as if he transcended the boundaries of time, revisiting the moments that once shaped his relationship. The laughter, the tenderness, the shared dreams – it all came back to the surface.

Ajay took a deep breath to ground himself in the moment. The memories served as a painful reminder of what was lost while also serving as an expression of the love that had once blossomed.

As Ajay sat there, immersed in his thoughts and memories, his phone buzzed, interrupting his contemplation, it was a call from his friend, Rocky.

"Hey Buddy," Ajay said

Rocky was excited "You won't believe it, but I managed to get some tickets of the concert in the city, I thought you and Priya might enjoy it. And I have a couple of extra ones so feel free to bring someone along."

A smiled emerged on Ajay, "That's great news buddy, Priya and I would love to come, anyways when is the concert?"

Ajay eagerly shared the details, "It's happening tonight, I'll drop the tickets at your place, it's going to be an amazing night."

They chatted a bit before ending the call.

When Ajay thought about inviting someone, naturally his mind drifted towards Priya, he knew that she had a fondness for music and it would be a perfect opportunity to spend some time together.

He immediately called Priya and shared all the details about the concert, Priya was excited when she heard that, she suggested that they also invite Shreya.

Before his memories could take him back in time, he somehow grounded himself in the present moment. he hesitated before responding, he wondered how Shreya would react about his presence. But one thing he knew was that it might be an opportunity to heal all the emotional wounds of his past.

"Can't wait to be with you again, Ajay" she said

"I feel the same way, Priya" he said

Later that evening all three of them found themselves at the concert, they stepped inside the concert hall.

They noticed that rocky was already waiting for them.

"Hey there, my friend." said Rocky, he rushed towards Ajay as he saw him.

Ajay was excited, "Hey, bro, we haven't seen each other in a while."

"Hi Priya, how are you?" Rocky said

"Hi, I'm fine, how about you?" It seems your friend's little tied up these days."

"I'm fine, and to be completely honest, the reason my friend is tied up is because he is about to tie the knot." Rocky said

Ajay and Priya couldn't contain their laughter.

"And you must be Shreya, Priya's sister, right?"

"Yeah." she shook hands with Rocky.

They talked for a while as there was still some time for the concert to begin, reminiscing about old times, shared laughter, and caught up on each other's lives.

The concert began, The three of them found a spot in the crowd, close enough to feel the music's pulse but with a comfortable distance between them. they found themselves immersed in the music, surrendering to its spellbinding allure. They danced, sang along, and lost themselves in the magic of the concert. Time seemed to slip away as they were enveloped In the melodies that resonated with their souls.

Amid all the chaos, Ajay and Shreya found a moment to converse. The vibrant lights illuminated their faces, casting colourful reflections in their eyes. Their conversation seemed like a bridge between past and present.

Ajay turned to Shreya with a warm smile, "What an amazing night! The concert is incredible."

Shreya nodded "Absolutely! I'm glad we're here, it feels like a lifetime since we last enjoyed a concert."

Ajay kept his silence for a moment and then he finally broke the silence "it's been quite a journey, We've come a long way since those days, haven't we?"

Shreya looked at him with a gentle smile on a corner of her lips, "Indeed Ajay, life has its own way of taking us on an unexpected journey."

Ajay's voice carried a touch of gratitude, his tone softened, "You're right, Shreya. We may have taken different roads, but I'm grateful you were a part of my life."

Shreya's eyes sparkled with understanding, "I feel the same way, Ajay."

There was a brief pause between them, as if they found solace in the silence, allowing their thoughts to take them away. Sometimes we have a lot of things to say, we just don't find the proper words.

Ajay finally broke the silence, "You know, Shreya, I still reflect on the moments we shared. The laughter, the tears, the ups and downs – everything shaped us over time."

Shreya's heart skipped a beat as she heard those words, emotions intwined with each moment she shared with him, she could feel the weight of those memories. In that moment it felt like she stood on the bridge between their past and present.

Taking a deep breath, she rooted herself in the present. "You're right Ajay, those moments we shared, were like the fragment of our story, each containing its own colour and depth."

Closing her eyes, a soft smile illuminated her face, she allowed herself to wonder through the corridors of the memories. She could almost feel the sweetness of their laughter and the warmth of their embrace.

She opened her eyes as she came back in the present moment, "The memories we shared will forever hold a special place in my heart."

"I understand, Shreya. It can be difficult to move on from what we once shared," Ajay said.

"Our journey may have taken a different turn, but I'm grateful for the love we once shared." A sense of calm washed over her as she spoke, she understood that her past was just a stepping stone to her present.

In that moment where she was caught up in the reflection and present, she found a newfound appreciation for the present moment. With each breath, she let go of the weight of the past and embraced the beauty of her life.

Throughout the concert they shared glances and smiles at each other, they started to savour the present moment they were sharing, their pain of the past slowly started to fade. As if the music itself was weaving new stories of their life.

Ajay and Shreya were engaged in their conversation, sharing stories about the past and cherishing the memories they had shared, their voices caught the attention of Priya and Rocky, who had been immersed in the music playing at the concert. they exchanged a knowing look and decided to join the conversation.

"Hey guys, what's up?" Priya said with a warm smile.

Shreya smiled back, "Oh, just going down memory lane and sharing some old stories. Nothing special, really."

Rocky smiled, "Well, sometimes those simple conversations turn out to be the most meaningful ones. Mind if we join you?"

"Sure, join us!" Ajay said

And just like that, the conversation expanded, they all shared hearted stories, it was a moment of togetherness where past and present intertwined.

it's been an amazing concert so far. The energy is off the charts! Rocky said as he was still a bit excited about his favourite song playing over the stage.

Shreya nodded, "Absolutely! I'm loving every moment of it."

The concert ended with some final chords; Ajay felt like the pain of the past was gradually fading away replaced by a growing sense of embracing the life. he discovered that the wounds of the past had gradually started to heal, leaving space for acceptance.

On the following evening, Ajay invited Priya to his home, as he wanted to spend more time with her.

They were standing in the balcony, a cozy space adorned with twinkling lights and colourful flowers. The soft wind played with her hair; she kept looking at the breathtaking view of the city.

In the midst of that Ajay was wondering about the honesty of his relationship, he wanted to share what he had been holding onto. He approached her, his eyes filled with a mix of nervousness, Her presence brought a sense of calm to his restless heart.

"Hey Priya, isn't the weather beautiful right now?" he said.

"Priya looked at him and smiled softly. "Absolutely, Ajay. There's something magical about the evening breeze. It's so soothing."

His mind was consumed by thoughts of his past. The weight of his emotions felt heavy, and he knew he couldn't keep things to himself any longer. He took a deep breath, gathering his courage, and decided it was time to talk to Priya.

"Priya, there's something I need to share with you. It's about my past, and I want to be completely honest with you." Ajay said

"What is it, Ajay? You can tell me anything," her eyes filled with concern.

Ajay took a moment to gather his thoughts, "Actually, Priya, I want to be completely honest with you. Before we met, I was in a relationship with Anjali. But as time went on, during my college days, I found myself drawn towards Shreya. We fell in love with each other, but eventually, we moved on," Ajay explained, his voice tinged with vulnerability.

Priya's expression softened, a mix of understanding and sadness crossing her face. She took a moment to process Ajay's words before responding.

"Ajay, I appreciate your honesty," she said, her voice filled with sincerity. "I need some time to process this information and figure things out."

Ajay nodded, he understood that it wasn't easy but he can't hide things from her either, he knew that she needed time and space to navigate her emotions.

"I understand, Priya," he said "You can take your time, I'm here for you, no matter what."

The evening sky turned into a canvas of hues, they remained enveloped in silence, the wind continued to blow carrying the weight of unspoken words, they knew that their conversation was creating a turning point in their relationship. Although the future remained a mystery to them, what they did know was that their journey was far from over.

Book 5: Faded Memories

Chapter – 9

Shreya felt at peace in the warm atmosphere that surrounded her in the comfort of her room. The room was illuminated by soft lighting. the shelves were holding her favourite novels and the walls were covered in pictures.

Seated on her bed, she noticed a stack of novels on a table close to her bed, which made her smile as they contained stories that remained unexplored, one of them had a bookmark between the pages – representing her recent engagement with the words.

Next to her, her laptop lay open on the bed, she noticed an old folder that contained some photographs from her collage days, amidst them there were few pictures of her with Ajay. As she went through those images, her heart was filled with warmth, her memories took her back In time, to the moments she shared with her, the laughter, the intimacy, the love – everything flashed before her eyes.

While she was reflecting on her faded memories, tears rolled up in her eyes. She could almost feel the warmth of his presence in them. the photographs brought with them a cascade of emotions.

Of all the things she missed about him – the one stood above the rest was his gentle touch, feeling a touch of his hand against her skin brought her the ineffable tenderness that melted her heart.

She longed for a moment when his fingers intertwined with hers creating a connection that transcended words. in those simple yet exquisite moments she felt an unspoken language that formed between them. she longed for the moments when his gentle touch would evoke a multitude of emotions.

She closed her eyes to immerse herself in those memories, she could almost feel the whispers of their conversation that fascinated the moon to illuminate the sky. the intimacy of the silence they shared enwrapped them in a blanket of comfort. Everything was vivid, everything was fresh again, everything was back on the surface again.

She wiped her tears, closed her laptop, she looked at her novels – wondering which one would help her cope with her loneliness.

Feeling a surge of longing for his presence, she reached her phone and called him. After what it felt like an eternity Ajay finally picked it up.

"Hello?" He answered.

"It's me, Shreya. She whispered her voice filled with a sense of vulnerability, "Can we meet? Just for a little while? There are things I need to talk.

Ajay hesitated for a moment; he could feel the weight of her emotions in those words. Shreya's heart kept racing as she was wondering if he'd pick it up.

Finally, Ajay agreed, "Alright Shreya! Let's meet."

Shreya experienced a wave of relief mixed with a jolt of anxiety. They chose a meeting time and location, a quiet café close to her collage.

After they ended the call, she kept wondering if the meeting would provide the closure, they needed, or would it deepen the emotional wounds she already had?

She looked for solace in the comforting embrace of novels. She gently picked up a book, she started engaging with the words which had transported her to a different realm's countless times before. she allowed herself to immerse in the narrative, hoping it would bring a temporary relief from the weight of her emotions.

Page after page hours melted away, she found a sense of relief in the narrative, something that allowed her to explore the depths of her emotions through someone else's perspective.

She finally closed the book, placing the bookmark so she could continue engaging with the it later, a sense of tranquillity washed over her, reading provided her the much-needed escape from the overwhelming waves of her own reality. She set the book aside as she waw trying to gather the strength to face her own narrative.

Through her room's window, Priya was watching the shining stars. The night sky stretched out over the horizon, like a vast canvas painted with countless stars.

Her mind kept replaying the scenario when ajay told her about his past relationships, his eyes reflected the pain he felt, the ups and downs of his relationships, the lessons he learned and the scars he carried.

She wondered if the feelings between them were genuine at all, was it built upon the strong foundation, or was it more like a fleeting moment in time? She knew that his past relationships had shaped the person he had become, but she wondered if there were hidden layers that remained uncovered.

In the midst of everything these was a sense of hope that refused to fade, she recalled the moments she spent with him, the conversations that flowed effortlessly, his presence made her feel alive.

She took a deep breath allowing the clouds of her thoughts to settle down. Priya longed for a sense of clarity, something that would bring a sense of calm amid the chaos of life.

Although she hadn't completely figured out everything yet, but she was willing to explore the depth of their bond. She knew that there was only one way she could ever bring that clarity – by meeting him.

"I can compare you to every single thing in the vast universe – nothing could ever comprehend what I feel for you" she thought.

She made a decision to confront her uncertainties head-on as she closed the window of her room. She was aware that communication was key in any relationship and that she couldn't let her doubts to develop if she kept them to herself. She wanted an open and sincere conversation with Ajay in order to get answers.

The next morning, Shreya found herself at the café where she used to meet him, taking a seat near the window, she gazed out at the world awakening to a new day, her mind filled with a swirl of thoughts and emotions.

Time seemed to have slowed down as she waited for him to arrive, with each passing moment, her heartbeats grew louder, echoing in the stillness of the café, she wondered if Ajay would show up or not.

Just when she was questioning her decision to meet him, the door of the café opened slightly and Ajay stepped inside, his eyes searching for her and vice versa. Their eyes met across the room, a mix of emotions flickering between them.

She closed her eyes and tried to focus on the present moment. for a moment, they simply looked at each other, as if they were searching for answers of their questions in the eyes. Although they stopped reading the book of their relationship, some chapters remain unfinished.

Shreya finally broke the silence.

"Hi, Ajay. It's good to see you." Shreya said.

"Hi, Shreya, good to see you too. I wasn't sure if you would want to meet after everything that happened." Ajay said.

"I needed closure, Ajay. There are things I need to say, and I hope we can find a way to move on." Shreya said.

"I feel the same Shreya, there are so many things I still want to say to you." Ajay said.

Shreya took a deep breath to collect her thoughts, "I want you to know that I don't have any resentments towards you, I'm forever grateful that we were together even for a little while, we made memories, even though they were just fleeting moments of life, I will continue to cherish the love we had even though it's just a thing of the past."

It seemed as if she was trying to hold her emotions, but the weight of them could be felt in her words, she was with him and yet her thoughts were miles away lost in the corridors of memories.

"I understand Shreya, we both find ourselves often going back to the memories of the past, I know that it's been a long time since we parted ways but it's not like we can suddenly stop ourselves from thinking about each other."

Her fingers traced the outline of her coffee cup as an attempt to ground herself in the present moment. she took a slow breath as if trying to calm the storm of thoughts within her.

"Please know that I didn't mean to hurt you." Ajay said.

"I believe it's time we accept what we once shared as a part of our past and move on in our life." Shreya said.

Tears rolled up in her eyes, she blinked them away regardless of the chaos she felt within her, she tried to maintain her composure.

"I'm grateful for everything we once shared – every single thought, feeling and experience." Shreya said.

"I'm grateful too Shreya. I hope we can find our happiness – now that our paths are different." Ajay said.

"I wish you all the happiness as well, Ajay. Thank you for listening to me." Shreya said.

"Thank you for sharing your thoughts with me. I will always remember our time together. Take care of yourself Shreya." Ajay said.

As their time drew to a closure, they realised that they needed space to heal themselves, although they shared something in the past, but they knew that they couldn't rewrite those chapters of their life.

Meanwhile at Priya's home, her parents were busy discussing about the marriage preparations as the date drew closer, her mom noticed that Priya wasn't paying much attention towards them, she was lost In her own thoughts.

Priya's mom reached out to her and set close to her, she took her hand and gently placed it between her palms, "Priya, what happened dear? You look a little off today, did something happen? you can talk to me dear." She smiled at her.

"I'm fine mom, it's just I'm worried about the preparations as much as you do." Priya said.

It looked as if she wanted to say something else, but she couldn't gather the words for it, she was wondering about the honesty of their relationship, she constantly found herself questioning Ajay in her own imagination, "Was everything between us ever real? since I met you, I've always felt like you are someone I never want to lose." I wanted to live with you until life allows me to. but sometimes you make me question everything."

"It's fine Priya, you don't have to worry about those things." Her mom said.

Those words helped Priya found a comfort amidst the turbulence of thoughts.

Priya went to her room excusing herself and closed the door, as she was lying on bed her mind replayed events, specifically the moments she spent with him.

Closing her eyes, she immersed herself in the memories, the moonlight sky they shared while they expressed their love towards each other. and yet, amidst her fantasies a wave of doubt was fading in, she questioned her own worthiness and wondered if she could ever be the person he needed.

The sound of the door opening interrupted her thoughts, and when she opened her eyes to see who was at the door, it was Shreya. she stepped inside with a bright smile on her face.

"You look happy today, Shreya. What's the secret?"

"Oh, it's nothing, Priya. Just enjoying the little moments of life." Shreya said

Priya couldn't quite unravel the true depth of Shreya's emotions. Shreya tried her best to put on a happy face to avoid involving others in her inner turmoil. Each day she had to struggle with the waves of sadness and longing, she would gather all her courage to supress her emotions, But it was a constant struggle. Her every waking moment was consumed by thoughts of their laughter, their late-night conversations, and their shared dreams.

On the other hand, Shreya already had an idea of what she was going through, it's simply not easy. Shreya went closer and sat beside her.

"You look upset, please tell me what happened?" Shreya said

"I... I don't know if I can... It's too complicated." She hesitated, unsure whether to burden Shreya with everything.

"Please, Priya, remember that I am here for you. You can count on me." Shreya said.

"Ajay told me about his past relationships", Priya tried to gather her words, she almost choked as she said that, The weight of his feelings felt almost unbearable. The truth he had shared about his past relationships felt like a heavy burden on her shoulders. The recollections of their time together, flooded her mind, intertwining with her present reality. She tried to gather her thoughts, her voice catching in her throat as she struggled to find the right words to respond to Shreya.

The intense quiet that followed filled the room and intensified Priya's internal turmoil. Her eyes wandered aimlessly, searching for solace in the familiar corners of her room. In the midst of the chaos that surrounded her, she yearned for clarity.

Taking a deep breath, Priya tried to steady her racing heart. She knew she needed to confront her feelings, to find the words that could express the depth of her inner struggle.

"I'm not upset with you Shreya. I didn't expect him to be in a relationship with you and keep it a secret all this time," she wiped her tears.

"I can relate with you Priya. Sometimes our emotions are just so attached that our memories continue to haunt us. I can only imagine how difficult it must have been for you to go through this." Shreya said.

Priya looked at her, "I know Shreya, I simply can't find a way not to think about him. I often find myself lost in thoughts, reflecting upon the memories that made, the stolen glances and the desire to pause the time when we were together."

"I've felt that before." Shreya smiled, hiding a havoc of emotions behind it. "Please know that I'm here with you." She held Priya's hand and caressed it gently.

Priya sat in silence, a warm smile appeared on her face, she could feel the depth of Shreya's emotional maturity, the way she let herself feel anything was really inspiring. She could see Shreya's vulnerability and openness of her emotions as they became apparent in her eyes.

Without saying a word, Priya leaned forward and enveloped Shreya in a warm embrace, she held her tightly, silently conveying her understanding though a simple gesture.

The silence in the room allowed them the space to process their thoughts and emotions at their own pace.

"Even though we were never meant to be together, we really had feelings for each other, didn't we? As if you were the main character of our story and yet it remains incomplete. Now that I think about it, I'm going to miss it all – that smell of coffee at your favourite café, our late-night conversation and your presence. Maybe you've stopped reading our story, but I will continue to write it, hoping that someday I might find comfort in those words," Shreya thought.

Chapter – 10

In his room, Ajay was by himself. The bedside lamp's gentle glow warmed the walls as he sat there. The clock's ticking indicated that time was running out. A wave of memories returned as soon as he saw Priya's photo in his phone's album; each picture was a priceless snapshot of his time spent with Priya.

He looked at the photographs, a bittersweet smile appeared at the corners of his lips. The pictures portrayed happy, humorous, and loving times when it seemed like they had the entire world at their fingertips. They had created an adorable bond between them that seemed unbreakable.

Ajay's thoughts took him back to their first meeting, he could imagine the way Priya's eyes sparkled with fascination as they got to know each other. He thought back on their shared experiences and the many hours they had spent talking. His affection for Priya grew as each memory brought up a different feeling.

He knew that there were some secrets between them, secrets that had only recently come to light.

His eyes were heavy with exhaustion, and it was clear that he hadn't gotten enough sleep. Each blink was an uphill battle against the exhaustion engulfing him, and yet in the midst of all that he couldn't escape from her thoughts.

Lying on his bed, Ajay replayed memories of their time together, soon he fell asleep.

In the realm of his dream, his mind painted a vivid image of their meeting, He found himself at the place they first met, it was early in the morning, the golden rays of the morning sun caressed Priya's face, highlighting it's features with a radiant glow.

"Ajay, I know this is an incredibly difficult decision for both of us", Priya said as she broke the silence between them, "But I can't seem to find a clear path forward."

Ajay's eyes were locked on Priya as he struggled to understand the significance of her choice as the realisation of the words that followed broke his heart.

"Priya, you don't have to face this alone. I'm here for you, no matter what," he said.

"I think it would be better if we continue our life in our own separate ways, it's not an easy choice, but I hope it will allow us to find ourselves and heal." Tears welled in Priya's eyes as she spoke.

Ajay could feel the depth of her words, he felt like everything fell apart in an instant, but still he gathered the courage to accept her words.

The dream gradually faded, Ajay woke up to the reality he was trying to escape – where he yearned for her presence. he could feel his heart racing, ajay looked at the clock and noticed it was 2:30 AM, he took a deep breath to ground himself in the moment to accept the realisation that it was just a dream.

Ajay woke up and glanced out the window. The city was quiet and everyone was asleep. The lights of the buildings twinkled softly, creating a peaceful scene against the dark sky. Ajay felt a sense of calm as he observed the stillness around him.

The quiet hours allowed him the space to think, standing there, looking at the sleeping city, Ajay made a silent promise to himself. He would take the necessary time to heal his emotional wounds, he knew that he would have to talk to her if he wanted to bring some clarity in their relationship.

he reached for his phone and dialled her number, hoping that her voice would bring him much needed comfort, the call continued to ring, his heart racing with anticipation, each passing ring felt like an eternity filling the silence of the room.

Ajay waited for Priya to answer his call, the phone continued to ring with no response. "I think she's asleep." He said to himself. Regardless of the reason, the absence of her familiar tone left him feeling even more unsettled. His failed attempt to connect with her ended up increasing a sense of worry. He sensed the distance widening between them as a result of the unanswered calls which intensified his inner chaos.

He sat his phone aside realizing that conversation would have to wait for a while, he realized that she needed her own space.

Meanwhile, Priya was still awake, the phone screen was stained with tears as she clenched it tightly in her hand. She decided not to respond to his calls, and it hurt her heart. Fear and guilt coexisted as she struggled to face the uncertain future that lay before her. Her mind raced, looking for answers that seemed to elude her with each passing second.

She sat there in silence, she couldn't stop herself from thinking about him, the comfort of her room felt suffocating, she longed for a sense of clarity amidst the chaos.

The burden of the circumstance continued to weigh heavily on Ajay's soul, causing his eyes to grow heavy with fatigue. He became exhausted as the minutes turned into hours. Ajay's eyes started to descend as he stared at the screen, he began to feel worn out from the inside out, and without even realising it, he fell into a restless sleep.

As the first rays of morning streamed through the window, Ajay's eyes fluttered open. He felt a renewed sense of determination and a burning desire to confront the challenges that lay ahead. he knew that the marriage date was drawing closer, he would have to talk to Priya about everything. He quickly got ready and rushed towards his car.

He accelerated through the familiar streets on his way to Priya's flat. His mind raced with thoughts as he anticipated the discussion that would follow. Ajay breathed in deeply as he approached her flat, gathering the courage to ring the doorbell. As he waited for Priya to respond.

The door swiftly opened revealing Shreya on the other side. Ajay's voice filled with surprise and genuine warmth as he greeted her, "Hi Shreya, how are you?"

Shreya's eyes widened in response to Ajay's unexpected presence, "I'm doing well, thank you. What brings you here?"

Ajay took a moment to compose himself, "Oh, I'm sorry. I actually wanted to talk to Priya."

Shreya smiled. "No worries, Ajay. Priya is actually still sleeping in her room. Please come, feel free to have a conversation with her, I know it must be Important."

With a quick gesture, Shreya invited Ajay inside her home. As they hurried through the hallway, Ajay noticed Anjali, deeply engrossed in her phone, seemingly oblivious to their presence. He was thankful that their parents weren't home at the moment.

Finally, he reached Priya's room. Ajay entered the room, his eyes falling upon her peaceful form, still lost in the realm of slumber. He approached her gently, mindful not to disturb her rest. Ajay quietly took a seat by her side, his eyes filled with a mixture of affection and concern.

As Ajay sat there, he carefully followed the lines and curves of Priya's face, trying to imprint each one in his mind. He watched her breath rise and fall and the soft tranquilly that surrounded her while she slept.

Priya's eyes fluttered open as Ajay's hand caressed her hair, and she was surprised to see him sitting by her side.

"What are you doing here?" Priya asked

"Actually, I wanted to talk to you, I've been trying to reach you out but it seems you won't answer my calls." He said

Priya's gaze dropped to the floor, her voice filled with a mixture of sadness and uncertainty, "I need time to process everything."

"We need to manage this stage of our lives as quickly as possible, Priya, as our wedding date is approaching." Ajay said

Priya's eyes welled up with tears as she tried to express her inner turmoil. "I need time to comprehend everything, Ajay. I'm struggling to process the fact that you were in relationship with both my sisters."

"Priya, as I told you before, I have moved on from the past." Ajay said

Priya looked at Ajay, her gaze searching for the truth in his words, "I don't know what to believe anymore, "I need time to sort through my feelings and figure out how to handle all of this."

Amidst the whirlwind of life, I want you to feel the unwavering support that I have for you. Your well-being truly matters to me, and I'll always be by your side, ready to lend a helping hand whenever you seek it." Ajay said

Feeling the weight of his thoughts, Ajay decided to give Priya the space she needed. But his mind was overwhelmed by all the things going on in his life, The complexity of his current relationship with Priya and their marriage, as well as memories of earlier relationships, continued to fill his thoughts.

Ajay turned to his friend Rocky for a way to express his feelings since he knew that their friendship may give him the relief and understanding he was looking for. He made a quick phone call to Rocky and decided to meet right away. He knew that he was the only friend he could turn to in times of difficulty.

Ajay picked up rocky and his presence brought a slight sense of comfort. Together, they embarked on a journey, hoping that through their conversation, Ajay would find clarity and the strength to navigate the situation he was in.

With a hint of annoyance in his voice, Ajay commented, "The traffic seems relentless today. His eyes caught the brightly coloured movement of traffic signals ahead as he glanced through the windscreen.

"Yeah, it's one of those days when traffic is at its peak." Rocky Said

There was silence in the car, as the signal turned to green, the traffic gradually began to ease, and Ajay seized the opportunity to accelerate the car forward.

Rocky broke the silence, his voice filled with empathy. "Ajay, I can sense that something's been bothering you. What's been going on?"

Ajay took a deep breath, his grip tightening on the steering wheel. "Rocky, it's about Priya. Even though the wedding is drawing closer, I still feel an immense amount of uncertainty. I have so many thoughts racing through my head, including worries, concerns, and even memories of previous relationships. I don't want to bring any unsolved issues into this marriage."

Rocky gave a sympathetic nod while keeping his attention on the path ahead. "I understand, Ajay. It's normal to have such doubts and concerns, especially when preparing to make a decision of this significance. Have you discussed your feelings with Priya?"

Ajay sighed and looked in the rearview mirror. "Still not. I want to have an honest conversation with her, but I'm worried about what it could possibly bring up. What if our paths are never meant to align?"

"It's a good thing that you're giving her the space to process everything, but remember there's only one way to bring some clarity and that's by trying to communicate with one another, as for your paths are meant to align or not, I can clearly see how much you guys care for each other." Rocky Said

Ajay's grip on the steering wheel loosened, his focus shifting back to the conversation at hand. "You're right, I need to talk to Priya, express my concerns, and listen to hers. We owe it to ourselves to address these doubts before taking such a significant step."

Rocky smiled, "Absolutely, Embrace the opportunity to have a genuine conversation with Priya, and trust that the timing will be just right."

Ajay noticed a glimmer of hope in Rocky's words as they continued their journey. As the burden on his shoulders started to lessen, a renewed resolve to speak openly with Priya took its place.

Later that day, Ajay found himself at home, the familiarity of his surroundings offering solace from the events of the day. He entered the living room and heard his parents talking animatedly about his wedding attire.

His mother, flipping through a catalogue of traditional outfits, spoke with excitement. "Ajay, we've been looking at some options for your wedding attire. What do you think of this embroidered sherwani?

He had been avoiding the subject for a while now, but he knew that he could no longer escape from it.

"Ajay. Your mother has an excellent eye for these things. We want you to select a perfect outfit for your wedding day. It's important to honour our traditions and make a memorable impression."

he took a deep breath, trying to gather his thoughts. "Dad, I've been searching for the perfect outfit, but I haven't found one that truly speaks to me yet. I'll keep looking, and I promise to find one before the wedding."

His mother seemed to have an idea how he might be feeling at the moment,

"Ajay, dear, your father and I understand the pressure you're under. Remember, it's your special day, and we want you to feel comfortable and happy. Take your time, but do let us know as soon as you find something you love." His mom said

"Sure, Let's consider a few options for the hotel, We can prioritize our loved ones for the main ceremony and then extend invitations to others for the reception. It will ensure that we share this special moment with everyone who means a lot to us," Ajay said.

"Ajay, I'm glad you understand the importance of including everyone. Let's start making a list of guests and reach out to the hotels immediately. We'll find the perfect place to celebrate your wedding, and with a bit of luck, we'll secure it for the wedding day." His father said

Ajay listened intently, appreciating his parents' efforts to make his wedding day special and their involvement. But his thoughts kept returning to the conversation he had with Rocky earlier in the day and the doubts that were still present in him.

Ajay's thoughts took him back to the day they met; he noticed how the simple things made her happy. Falling in love is really about finding the little things to cherish. Especially when you look back at those moment, it's those little things that make a lasting impression.

He quickly snapped back to the present moment as the discussion continued, Ajay's anxiety slowly turned into excitement. Together with his parents, he knew that they could navigate the remaining preparations and make the wedding a memorable event.

As his father brought up Priya in their conversation, Ajay's eyes widened in surprise. What did you just say, Dad?" You had a conversation with Priya? He asked, feeling confused and surprised at the same time.

"Yes, Ajay, I had a conversation with Priya today. She's a remarkable girl, and I can see why you like her so much."

Gathering his thoughts, Ajay leaned forward, his eyes locked with his father's. "Dad, what did you and Priya discuss? I didn't expect you to reach out to her. What did she say?"

"She told me that she and her family are going to the mall tomorrow to finalize her wedding dress."

Ajay's mind was racing with a mix of anxiety and anticipation. "Tomorrow? That's too soon! I'm can't wait to see her and discuss about a few things. Life feels really hectic these days, I have to pay attention to the preparations and at the same time I have to find a way to have an honest conversation with Priya."

Ajay went to his room, his heart pounding with anticipation and excitement, he dialled her number, yearning for her voice to provide the comfort he sought. He was left wondering why Priya wasn't answering his texts or calls. Was she busy? Or perhaps, was she avoiding him?" Feeling helpless, Ajay decided to send Priya a text message, hoping that she would respond. He typed out his concerns, expressing his worry and asking her to let him know if everything was alright. The minutes felt like hours as he anxiously waited for a reply, his imagination running wild with the worst-case scenarios.

We worry too much about others because we really care for them, but sometimes no amount of overthinking or worrying can provide the control over how the events unfold.

Next day at the mall, Priya and her family explored the racks of stunning wedding dresses as they strolled through the busy mall. Priya couldn't help but feel a tinge of sadness despite the palpable excitement in the air. She yearned to find the ideal dress, one that would make her heart sing, but nothing grabbed her attention so far.

Priya tried on various dresses one by one, and Shreya eagerly offered her opinions, but she knew in her heart that their words couldn't make up for her own unhappiness. Her father was eager to see her in the wedding dress, so she put on a fake smile.

As she emerged from the changing room, her father's eyes lit up with anticipation. "Priya, my dear, it looks great on you, what do you think?" he asked, excitement dancing in his voice.

"It's nice, dad," she replied, her voice tinged with forced cheerfulness. "But, you know, I want something that truly reflects the essence of wedding rituals." Priya said.

"Priya, we want you to feel radiant and beautiful on your special day. Let's checking the other ones we might find the one that suits you."

Priya nodded, feeling grateful for her mother's help and compassion. They entered the store further, looking around every corner for the elusive gown with renewed vigour. As time passed, Priya's heart grew heavy and her disappointment increased.

she put the dress on with her heart pounding in anticipation. A sincere smile gradually grew across her face as she looked at herself in the mirror. This was it—

the outfit that reflected her distinct sense of style and personality and spoke to her soul.

"Priya, my dear, you look absolutely stunning," her father said, his voice filled with admiration. "This is the one, without a doubt."

As the sun begins to set, they stepped out from the mall, everyone gets into the car, but Anjali told them that she had some work and she'd be late. Shreya looked out of the window; a light breeze was rustling in her hair. she could sense mixed feelings in the air, something that compelled to break the silence.

"Dad, you seem to be enjoying life as Priya's wedding approaches. What's making you feel so joyful?" Shreya asked.

Glancing at her, her father's smile widened before he shifted his attention back to the road. With a sense of fond reminiscence, he responded, "You're right, Shreya. I can't help but feel immense joy as I witness Priya embarking on this new chapter of her life. It's a beautiful moment, and it fills my heart with happiness."

Her father paused for a moment before continuing, his voice carrying a faint undertone of sadness. Priya's marriage has made it clear that she won't be staying with us for very long, as you can see. She is about to leave her home and begin a family of her own. Not only Priya, but also you and Anjali would go back to

Canada soon, he added, his voice tinged with both pride and longing.

He continued to navigate the city streets, and found himself immersed in the bustling rhythm of urban life.

"You're right, dad, Priya didi would also move to Canada after the marriage." Shreya said.

"Yes, my son-in-law is a wonderful person," he replied, his voice filled with admiration. "I am grateful to have him as part of our family."

Priya could see the flow of the city's energy through the windscreen. Streetlights glowed brightly as pedestrians hurried along sidewalks, businesses displayed their goods, and the night sky was illuminated. Despite the difficulties she was experiencing inside her own heart, the world around her was still thriving. It was a symphony of life.

"Shreya, I must confess that a few weeks ago, while we were having dinner at the hotel, I said accidentally that I would feel lonely while both of my daughters were in Canada. But I had no idea that my son-in-law was listening carefully."

You know what he said to me Shreya? He said, "Uncle, you don't have to bear that burden alone. I am also your son, and if you had shared your feelings with me earlier, I would have surely reconsidered my decision. Family comes first."

Priya's father looked at her and continued to talk while also keeping his eyes on the road ahead, "Priya, I must say your future husband is very mature. I can see that he's the perfect match for you."

As they arrived home, the echoes of their heartfelt conversation lingered in Priya's mind. The house greeted them with a familiar warmth, but the words exchanged in the car continued to resonate within her. She couldn't help but reflect on the love and unity that defined their family. Priya reached for her phone and sent a heartfelt message to Ajay, expressing her gratitude. The words flowed from her heart as she thanked him for his understanding and compassion, acknowledging the role he played in their family's bond.

"Hey Ajay, I wanted to thank you from the depths of my heart. Your support and consideration mean everything to me and my family."

Ajay was working and after a while, he was happy as soon as he saw Priya's message and he immediately replied, "I knew that you would forgive me and agree to the marriage."

Priya immediately replied, "I never said that Ajay, I still need time and space."

Book 6: Whispered Feelings

Chapter – 11

June 2023, 2 Week Before Marriage

Anjali was lost in thought as she stood by the side of the road when she heard an engine start to screech. She looked up to see a bike approaching, and as it got closer, she could identify the rider.

With a big smile on his face, he parked the bike and jumped off, walking towards Anjali with excitement evident in his eyes. Without wasting a moment, he wrapped Anjali in a warm, unexpected embrace. Surprised but pleased, she wrapped her arms around him, feeling the familiar comfort of his presence.

"I've been waiting for you, and you weren't answering my calls either." she said

"I'm so sorry my love, but here I am," he said.

"So, what's the plan for the evening? She asked a hint of excitement in her voice."

"Well, we're going to the kankariya lake, Let's take a ride and make this evening unforgettable," he said.

Anjali's eyes widened with surprise and delight. Kankaria Lake, holds innumerable memories of his college days. It had been years since they had last visited, and the mere thought of returning there with him filled Anjali's heart with joy.

"I've missed Kankaria so much, and it'll be amazing to experience it again with you," she said.

Anjali wrapped her arms around Her's waist as they hopped on the bike, holding on tightly as they sped through the busy streets. As they rode, the wind ruffled their hair, and their shared bond was rekindled by their laughter.

After reaching Kankaria, they parked the bike and strolled hand in hand along the lake's promenade. The vibrant lights reflected on the water's surface, casting a magical glow. They reminisced about their memories, sharing stories and laughter, relishing each moment together.

"Do you think it's time to share our love story with everyone?" he asked, his voice filled with anticipation.

"No, not yet," she said, her tone cautious. "I understand your eagerness, but we must proceed with caution. I know how you feel, but I'm willing to take these steps for the sake of our marriage," she assured him, her determination shining through her words."

"Do you think your father will approve of our idea of getting married?" Rocky asked

She took a deep breath, gathering her thoughts. "I will talk to Ajay about our relationship, but not right now. After their marriage, both Priya and Ajay will stand by us and support our relationship."

"I can't imagine what he'd say when he would come to know about this." He said

"Please don't worry my love, I'll take care of everything." She said

Rocky smiled warmly, his eyes gleaming with affection. "Anjali, our love means the world to me. This evening was just a small reminder of how precious our bond is. Let's promise to make more time for each other, to cherish moments like these, no matter how busy life gets."

A smile emerged across her face as he looked at her, realizing it was his playful way of expressing his affection for her. "Only we know how everything happened in our favor."

"Yeah, everything unfolded according to our plan." Rocky said

Both of them leaned in closer, their lips met, sealing their unspoken emotions with a passionate kiss. Time seemed to stand still as their bodies pressed closer, their hearts beating in synchrony.

Anjali and Rocky sat by the lake admiring the beautiful evening. They felt a deep sense of satisfaction knowing that their unexpected adventure had resulted in a wealth of lifelong memories.

"So, have you thought about how you'd help your friend and my sister forget about the past and focus on their present, I don't like to see them suffer anymore," she asked.

"Yeah, I have thought about something but there's only one way to solve everything – an honest conversation," said Rocky.

"I don't think Priya would even agree to meet him." she said.

"You're there to help her, aren't you?" Rocky smiled

"Of course, I'll talk to her." She smiled back.

As he dropped her off at her home, he turned to her with a warm smile and said, "See you tomorrow." The words carried a gentle promise, a reassurance that their connection would continue to grow.

"Yeah, see you tomorrow," she said, her voice carrying a mix of excitement and anticipation.

They parted with a final glance, knowing that the next day would bring new conversations, special moments, and a better understanding of their growing relationship. An inner sense of contentment settled within him as he drove away.

The next morning, Anjali finished her breakfast, she had a clear idea of how she would convince Priya to meet Ajay. Feeling energized and excited, she knocked onto Priya's room, only to notice that it was already open. she stepped inside, Anjali saw that Priya's clothes were neatly arranged on the bed. She heard the sound of water from the bathroom indicating that Priya was taking a shower. She picked a dress from her wardrobe the one Ajay gifted her on their engagement.

Anjali quickly composed herself and found a spot to sit, casually holding the dress beside her.

Moments later, Priya came out of the bathroom, her face lighting up with a surprised expression as she noticed Anjali sitting there. Without wasting any time, Anjali handed over the dress to Priya, While Priya was getting ready, Anjali seized the opportunity to grab her mobile phone and open WhatsApp. Her heart was beating faster as she texted ajay from Priya's phone, "It's been a long time since we saw each other. Let's meet up at Kankaria Lake in an hour. Oh, and Anjali will be coming with us too."

"What are you doing with my phone?" Priya asked.

"Oh, it's nothing." Anjali quickly closed all the apps and gave it back to Priya.

Priya had a strange feeling, since Anjali never checked her phone.

"How many days has it been since you considered spending some time outside?" Anjali asked, hiding her excitement behind a serious look.

"Nothing much just a week or two, but you know what I'm dealing with, its simply not easy for me to just forget everything." Priya said.

"You're right, it isn't. let's head out. today and you'll realise how insignificant your problems are" Anjali said.

"What, where are we going?" Priya asked as she was surprised.

"You don't have to worry about that, leave it all to me." Anjali quickly grabbed the car keys holding Priya's hand and nudging her towards the main door.

After they settled into the car, Anjali quickly messaged rocky, "My part is done, now it's your turn."

Rocky on the other hand, read her message and took a moment to craft a perfect excuse to get Ajay to come outside and meet him. He knew he had to make it sound convincing. He picked up his phone and dialled Ajay's number.

"Hey, Ajay! How have you been?"

"Hey Rocky, I'm good, what about you?"

Rocky quickly thought of a creative way to entice Ajay to join him.

"Listen, Ajay, you won't believe what I just discovered. There's this incredible new restaurant that has recently opened up. They offer mouthwatering dishes that are not only budget-friendly but also incredibly tasty. I can't wait to give it a try, and I thought it would be awesome if we could experience it together. What do you say? Let's meet there in an hour, It's been way too long!"

"That sounds amazing, Rocky! I'm in. I'll be there in an hour." He eagerly agreed

Priya and Anjali left in the car, their car skidding along the familiar roads. atmosphere inside the car was filled with a mixture of anticipation and uneasiness as Anjali told that they were going to meet Ajay.

Priya's mind whirled with a whirlwind of thoughts and feelings. The memories of the good times she had with Ajay mixed with her pain, leaving her torn between curiosity and caution. She wanted to meet Ajay but was afraid that what would she do in front of Ajay.

Ajay was shocked to see Rocky waiting at the main gate as he was just starting his car. He didn't waste any time in accelerating towards Rocky and told him to get in.

After a brief exchange of words, Ajay couldn't contain his curiosity and asked, "So, what about that new restaurant you mentioned earlier?"

Rocky fell silent for a moment, locking eyes with Ajay before finally speaking up, "I'm sorry, but we're not actually going to the restaurant. We're going to meet Priya."

Ajay's jaw dropped in shock upon hearing this unexpected revelation. It had been a while since he and Priya had spoken, especially after he had opened up about his past relationships. He wasn't sure how she would react upon seeing him again. Lost in his thoughts, Ajay's attention was abruptly diverted by a notification on his phone. It was a message from Priya, received half an hour ago, asking him to meet her.

Finally, Priya and Anjali reached Kankaria Lake, a well-known location humming with activity. In order to find a good spot to wait for Ajay to arrive, they parked the car in the designated parking lot close to gate number three. The anticipation hung in the air, fuelling Priya's nervousness and quickening her heartbeat. Each second felt longer than the previous one as the minutes passed. Priya's eyes swept the area, eagerly looking for a familiar face among the crowd. After what seemed like an eternity, she finally saw Ajay moving in their direction along with Rocky.

As their distance decreased, their heats raced, they locked their eyes for a while as if they found all of their answers in them. Their memories – both joyous and painful, flooded back on the surface, creating a whirlwind of emotions inside of them, making it harder to find the right words.

A faint smile appeared on her face as he approached her, Priya's heart raced as memories flooded back, a heartfelt symphony of smiles, tears, and special times spent together. She couldn't help but experience a wave of nostalgia for the moments they had spent together, longing and trepidation dancing in her heart.

Ajay, too, felt a rush of emotions as he gazed at Priya, he wondered if all those memories and feelings still remain between them or have faded into the sands of time. The rush of the crowd at the place simply faded away, as if the destiny itself wanted to give them a moment of their own.

Rocky, who had been standing nearby, interrupted with a touch of frustration, "So, you guys don't want to talk, right? Fine then." His words hung in the air, creating a momentary tension.

Ajay, feeling compelled to break the silence, turned towards Priya with a gentle smile and said, "Hey, Priya. How have you been?"

She felt a wave of relief wash over her as she responded, "Ajay, I've been doing well, navigating through life's twists and turns. How about you?"

Ajay's eyes softened as he replied, "I've had my fair share of ups and downs too, but I'm finding my way. It's comforting to see a familiar face amidst the chaos."

After a moment of comfortable silence, during which Priya and Ajay relished the feeling of reconnection, Ajay broke the quietude with a question that carried weight and significance.

"By the way, Priya, have you bought the wedding dress?" Ajay asked, his voice filled with curiosity.

She hesitated for a while, not knowing how to respond. The wedding dress, a symbol of commitment and plans for the future, now holds a different meaning.

Gathering her thoughts, Priya replied softly, "Yes, I have."

Rocky, realizing he was no longer needed, quietly excused himself, leaving Ajay and Priya to have a conversation. Anjali too decided to excuse herself allowing them a moment alone.

Their eyes remained locked for a while, as if they had discovered a comforting solace in each other's gaze. allowing them to silently communicate a myriad of emotions that words could not fully capture. It was as if their eyes held the remnants of a once-familiar world, inviting them to revisit the memories and feelings they had shared.

So many unspoken words lay dormant in his heart, waiting for the right moment to find their voice.

Unable to resist the urge, they embraced each other, their bodies closing the distance together, in that embrace their unspoken words found their voices. The rush of their emotions flooded their souls, her eyes filled with tears as they broke the embrace.

"I've always loved you Ajay, there hasn't been a single day without a thought of yours." Priya said.

"I too feel the same way Priya, I feel like I can't live without you." Ajay said

"I know Ajay but there are still things that I still haven't figured out yet, I really need some space, I know our marriage date is closer than before, my feelings for you still remain the same." Priya said.

Ajay nodded, showing that he understood what she said, but behind her words there was a deeper meaning, as if there was a room that remain unexplored. Which brought along a sense of sadness. But he was grateful that they met and talked, even for a little while.

Our lives are filled with these moments that seem fleeting when we're living them but later on, we realise they left a lasting imprint, sometimes after months or years we listen to something or read something and we start connecting the dots of how it all happened.

Rocky and Anjali were sitting comfortably in the garden and having fun as they left Ajay and Priya alone. The sun was shining brightly overhead, casting a warm glow on the vibrant flowers and lush green grass. The air was filled with the sweet scent of blossoms, creating a delightful atmosphere. As they were talking and laughing, Rocky held Anjali's hand and pulled her closer. The warmth of his touch sent a tingling sensation through her body, and she looked into his eyes, her heart skipping a beat.

"You know Anjali we won't be able to spend time with each other once you go to Canada again," Rocky said.

"I know right? It hurts but I don't have a choice, also it would take me almost a year before I return to India," she said.

"This garden pales in comparison to the beauty you bring into my life. Every moment spent with you is like a fairytale," Rocky said.

"I feel the same way." She smiled entwining her fingers with him.

"Anjali, I promise to cherish and protect the love we share," Rocky whispered.

"The way you care for me and express your commitment fills me joy," she said.

Rocky and Anjali found comfort and a strong connection in that instant, amidst the wonder of nature and the blossoming of their love, which would continue to grow.

After a while, rocky and Anjali went back to Ajay and Priya. They overheard her saying something, "Ajay it's a once in a lifetime decision for me, don't get me wrong I care about you, It's just that it's not easy for me."

"I understand, please know that what I feel for you is real, I'll continue to cherish our love till the end of time." Ajay said.

It seemed as if they wanted to talk a lot about their underlying issues but couldn't find the rights words to convey.

Rocky and Anjali exchanged meaningful looks, acknowledging that the issue persisted, yet there was a slight improvement for Priya and Ajay. While their encounter had sparked a ray of hope, they understood that resolving the underlying problems would be challenging.

After a while they parted ways, Priya and Anjali settled into the car, and drove off. As Anjali drove the car, Priya sat in silence, her unspoken words carrying weight. Sensing an underlying issue, Anjali promptly inquired about what they talked about, Priya began recounting the events, and with each passing moment, a wave of sadness washed over Anjali. But somehow, she managed to contain her feelings.

After an hour they both reach home. Shreya was having her lunch, Anjali and Priya sat on the couch, taking a moment to breath. "Where were you all this time?" said her mom.

"We were busy with some work mom, anyways I'm starving please bring me some of your delicious food," said Anjali.

"Sure, my dear." Said her mom

Priya's mind remained consumed by a whirlwind of thoughts and memories, kept replaying the interactions she had with Ajay. She was struggling to find her way through the depths of confusion and longing as she became lost in a sea of feelings.

Meanwhile, Ajay and Rocky were at McDonald's sat across from each other at a cozy corner booth. The aroma of freshly cooked food filled the air, The restaurant was bustling with customers, adding to the vibrant atmosphere. Rocky, known for his appetite, ordered both a juicy burger and a sizzling pizza. He eagerly dug into his food, savoring each bite, Ajay on the other hand seemed to be lost in thought, his face covered with sadness,

Rocky noticed him and asked, "Ajay, you've been quiet the whole time, what happened?" Rocky asked.

"I tried talking to Priya," he said, "but it was like we talked the least about things that bothered us the most. There's not much time left for our wedding, and Priya isn't sure we should go ahead with it or not."

"Listen, Ajay, Rocky began, "marriage is a big commitment, and it's completely natural to have doubts or uncertainties especially in the initial phases. It's important to have open and honest communication with Priya."

"I agree with you, I tried to do the same but sometimes it feels like nothing's working in my favour, as if we were never meant to be together."

"You don't have to feel that way, it's like one of those obstacles holding you back, and you've had troubles even worse than this."

Ajay took a moment to reflect on those words, somehow what rocky said was true, he went through so many things in the past something that shaped him and made him better.

"So, then what should I do now?" Ajay asked.

"You already know what you should do, you just have to find a way to do it." Rocky said as he savoured a large slice of his pizza.

"Maybe I should give her a call and discuss everything." Ajay said.

"That's not a good idea, why don't you guys meet each other somewhere alone? take her to her favourite place, this time I won't be around." Rocky said

"That's a great idea, I'll definitely try this out and see if it works."

They continued their conversations as they savoured the flavours. Every bite and sip added something new to their conversation, combining the excitement of discovering new tastes with the comfort of sharing the experience.

Meanwhile Priya was in her room, observing the sunset sky and it's vibrant colours. The soft evening breeze gradually interrupted the tranquillity of the evening. She took her diary which was on her table beside the bed, at first, she kept looking at the diary and the pages of it, she had a hobby of keeping a diary, but it's been a long time since she wrote anything down. the last thing she wrote was a few months ago, she couldn't help but smile as she went through the pages. "Writing gives you a space to express things, it's like a comfortable conversation you have with yourself." She said to herself.

She went to the window again looking at the tranquil evening as the sun continued to pain the orange hues on the sky. she took a moment to think about what to write, there only one thing that kept whirling around her mind – her relationship.

"I still remember the day when we first met, she wrote, at first, I was nervous I didn't know what I would even talk about, I sat in a cosy corner of the café and waited for you to arrive constantly looking around to find the familiar face amidst the crowd. And then you stepped inside, not just in the café – but in my life as well. while I don't remember what I thought about when I first saw you, but I knew I felt a sense of comfort in your presence, I felt like we were old friends, I really liked the way you talked about your ambitions and dreams along with the struggles you faced, I was really confused what to say, when you told me that you've been in a relationship before, as I've never been in one. Especially when our fingers intwined, I knew that fate wanted us to be together, your touch brought along a magical sense of happiness. That day you became my definition of love and affection."

She took a pause, looked at the sky again to collect her thoughts, she observed how the tree leaves would move along the gentle wind, the birds flying over the sky. she allowed her thoughts to wonder high above the sky.

"At this point of my life, she began to write, I don't know how the events would unfold. but I still long for your touch – the same one that once made me happy. In those moments when we were together, it felt like everything in life was perfect. I still feel the need for your presence. but it feels like meeting you was just another fleeting moment of life and now destiny is carving different paths for us as if we were never meant to stay together. I know that nothing external could fill the void in my heart."

Tears started to roll down from her eyes, she wiped a tear drop on the page as she continued to write, "I've started to question myself, were we ever meant to be together? I often find myself lost in thoughts – and you are the one I think about all the time, it feels like without your presence in it, the canvas of my life has lost all the colours."

She couldn't stop herself from crying anymore, each thought of him struck a chord in her heart, and amidst all that she wanted to assign words to those feelings, although It was difficult but she found a space to express her thoughts and feelings – by writing them down.

"I wonder if I should completely forget about your past and move on with our present, but the thought of you indulging in a relationship with someone so close to me – continues to haunt me, but I do know that what I feel for you has its own depth – something beyond the words."

She wiped her tears, put down her pen and closed the diary. The sky was gradually turning dark as the sun started to fade away behind the clouds. The calm ambience allowed her to embrace the moment, providing a sense of comfort amidst the havoc of her emotions.

She noticed her phone screen was still on, and there was a notification, she took her phone, it was a WhatsApp message from Ajay.

"Hey, can we meet? Somewhere alone?" the message read.

Priya took a moment before typing her reply, "sure, let's meet."

"Great, see you tomorrow."

"Yeah, see you tomorrow."

She turned off her phone and put it aside, "sometimes, against everything we all hope – that things will get better." She thought. While there was a growing anticipation to see him, she had a feeling that the meeting might intensify the cracks in their relationship, it might end up making things worse than they actually are, and yet she was yearning for his presence to feel that affection one more time.

Chapter – 12

The following morning, Ajay meticulously prepared himself, wanting to make a good impression and show her the depths of his commitment. He struggled to shake the mixture of excitement and anxiety that was whirling around inside of him as he got dressed. He stepped into his car and drove to Priya's apartment, He wanted nothing more than to bridge the gap between them, to heal any wounds caused by his past. he wanted her to express her thoughts and feelings so he could absorb all her pain allowing her the space to feel good.

He rehearsed his words carefully as he stopped the car at the parking area, and took the steps toward her door.

Priya was surprised as she opened the door only to see him standing Infront of her.

"Hey, how are you?" he said with a hint of nervousness.

"I'm good," Priya said.

"If you're ready, we can go," he said.

"Yeah sure." She said as the two of them walked towards the parking area.

They stepped inside the car without speaking anything, except that he told her to wear the seatbelt.

The journey towards their destination was mostly silent, they occasionally looked at each other, most of the time they didn't say anything, it was when they were waiting for the traffic signal to turn green, Priya broke the silence.

"So where are we going anyway? She asked.

"You'll know it soon." He said.

Words seem to fail each of them attempted to express their feelings, Each glance held a depth of longing and the desire to bridge the gap between their hearts. The silence felt uncomfortable and yet it became the canvas to pain their emotions.

After waiting for a while, the signal turned green and Ajay started driving, he looked at her and said, "We're almost there." Ajay's voice carried a sense of hope, as if he was ready to face whatever lay ahead of him. deep down he wanted her to be happy with whatever decision they end up making.

Ajay and Priya reached their destination, it was the river front, the place where it all began.

Ajay and Priya strolled along the serene riverfront, their footsteps in sync with the gentle rhythm of the flowing waters. The ambiance carried a sense of familiarity and nostalgia.

Ajay couldn't help but smile as he looked at Priya, "Remember, this is the place where we first met." His eyes sparkled as he tried to recollect what he felt on that day.

She nodded and looked at him, "Yes, I remember it." Her fingers tried to adjust her hairs as the wind played with them.

Ajay's voice held a touch of nostalgia as she tried to collect his words, "I can still vividly picture you standing right here, your hair dancing in the wind, and your smile that captivated me from the very first moment."

"It feels like it was only yesterday," she said in a softer tone, her voice carrying a gentle undertone of gratitude and vulnerability.

Ajay tried to gather the courage to say the words he was holding in his heart, "Priya, there's something I need to say... I want to apologize for the pain and confusion my past relationships have caused you."

She listened intently; her heart open to his words.

Ajay continued, "I realize now that my past actions have left scars on our relationship. I never intended to hurt you or make you question my commitment towards you. I was lost in my own journey, trying to find my place, and I failed to recognize the impact it had on us."

Deep down he knew that he can never change his past, but he can shape the future.

Priya took a moment to collect her thoughts, "I understand Ajay, you had your past – just like any other person. It hasn't been easy for me too." Her fingers naturally intwined with his and she felt the comfort she had been longing for.

Tears rolled up in Ajay's eyes, "The core idea of the relationship is that two people can feel a sense of happiness in each other's presence, but I guess I failed at it, at some point I felt like maybe we shouldn't have met."

They came to a halt, and Priya gently let go of his arm. She placed her palm against his face and said, "Look at me Ajay, I know how you feel, I'm happy with you. In fact, no one in the entire world can bring me the amount to happiness I feel when I am with you. She started crying, I... I don't have the words to express how much I've loved you; I've yearned for your presence in each moment when I was away from you."

They stood there immersed in each other's presence, the dark clouds gathered above the sky, and then the raindrops delicately kissed their skins. The raindrops were barely noticeable at first, but soon they enveloped the entire place into soft mist. It seemed like raindrops became the metaphor for washing away their pains allowing them a fresh start.

Ajay reached for Priya's hand and pulled her closer to him, they stood there drenched in the cascade of rain. Their eyes remained locked, as they embraced nature's symphony. Amidst the rainfall their lips closed the distance, softly brushing against each other, the sweetness of their kiss merged with the freshness of the rain creating an ethereal experience for the two of them.

The rain continued to pour around them completely soaking their clothes. They surrendered to the evoking emotions and the intensity of their passionate kiss, seeking comfort in each other's arms.

While they were sharing their kiss, something unfolded within Priya's mind, amidst the touch of their lips, Priya had a sudden visualisation.

In her visualisation, she could sense the couple that she dreamt of before, their presence was more vivid than before, the rain continued to cascade around the couple, they stood there in each other's embrace while being completely drenched in the rain, but this time their faces were slightly visible, she tried to dive deep into the vivid pictures, she felt as if the threads between her reality and dream were intertwined in some way.

what struck her the most was that she was having a similar kind of experience but the hard part was that — she never kissed him in the rain before, she could feel losing her focus slightly as she loosened her arms around Ajay.

Priya's thoughts drifted back and forth between the passionate kiss she shared with Ajay and the dream, trying to capture intricate details of the couple.

There was a sudden thunderstorm in the sky above them as they stood there at the river front, the couple in her imagination completely vanished their lips parted ways and she was completely moved for a moment, She immediately pulled herself back together.

She didn't say anything for a while, Ajay was wondering about what might have happened with her, he never saw her like that before — as if she was completely moved by something but he couldn't quiet figure out what it was.

She tried to focus back on those pictures she saw before, but she couldn't quite figure out who the dream couple were, as if they were close and yet remained elusive.

"What happened Priya?" Ajay said.

"No, it's nothing, Just let it go." She said her voice cracking in between.

Priya's heart quickened as she tried to make sense of what just happened.

Ajay reached for her hand, trying to provide a sense of comfort.

"Priya, you can tell me about it? Is something bothering you?" He asked.

Just as she was about to speak her mind wondered towards another visualisation. This time, the rain had stopped, and she could see their favourite café's familiar surroundings. it was the same café where she and Ajay usually meet, as she tried to focus on the details she was shocked by the revelation, she saw a couple but their faces were clearly visible – they were Ajay and Shreya.

Priya experienced a wave of conflicting feelings. She was shocked, confused, and slightly uncomfortable as her heart raced.

"I think we should leave, I'm sorry I don't mean to be like this, I feel lost and confused Ajay, I don't have words to clearly explain everything.

Ajay was wondering what might have happen to her, he was about to say something but she interrupted him.

Taking a deep breath, Ajay looked into Priya's tear-filled eyes, he's been trying to suppress his feeling of frustration from a long time.

Ajay turned towards Priya, his voice laced with a hint of anger and frustration."I've tried to explain this to you so many times, Priya. I've moved on from that relationship, and it's been years since our lives took different paths."

"I want to build a future with you Priya, I want to wake up next to you and cherish the love we share."

He paused before saying anything, "Shreya and I were in a relationship back when we were in collage, we met and fell in love – it all seemed to happen instant and yet it was ephemeral at the same time. We last spoke a few weeks ago and decided to go our separate ways from there."

"Do you want to know why we parted ways? She decided to go abroad for her studies and I told her that we won't be able to maintain our long-distance relationship. We both decided to part ways on the very spot we first met."

Ajay yearned for solutions, urgently seeking understanding amidst the emotional storm that constantly consumed him. He yearned for Priya to understand the suffering he had gone through, to feel sympathy for the broken parts of his heart.

He kept trying to explain things to Priya, but she could not get rid of the flashbacks of Shreya and Ajay's past. Ajay on the other hand couldn't distance himself from her.

He wanted her to grasp the magnitude of his suffering, to extend a hand of understanding and compassion. Their future hung in the balance, waiting for the choice they would make—to either heal the wounds that had been inflicted or let the storm of resentment tear them apart forever.

Priya struggled to speak as her own feelings began to surface. Her voice trembled. She found it difficult to put into words the depth of her regret and pain she felt for the suffering she had unknowingly brought on.

Tears started flowing from her eyes, it was the first time he raised his voice against her, but he wasn't completely at fault either, both of them were attempting to navigate the complexities of life – but this time it seemed as if their choices in life unfolded the events they were experiencing. If only they had this idea that eventually everything would connect in its own complex ways, things would have been better – but to our surprise life has its own miraculous way of unfolding events.

The rain gradually subsided, leaving them both completely soaked and enveloped in the silence once again. They made their way back to the car, water dripping from their hair and clothes. An almost tangible silence accompanied them on their way to Priya's house. mirroring the weight of their unspoken thoughts and emotions.

Each passing streetlight was casting fleeting shadows upon their faces, mirroring the complexities of their relationship. Ajay stole a quick glance at Priya as he looked for any sign of acceptance or understanding. In the midst of his rage, he yearned for a connection between them, a bridge that would help them get through the difficulties that lay ahead.

He dropped her home, he hoped that she would turn around to say something but she didn't.

Later that evening, as the weight of the day settled upon Ajay's shoulders, regret washed over him like a relentless tide. He found himself replaying the words he had spoken to Priya.

Sitting alone in the quiet solitude of the balcony, Ajay's thoughts swirled with a mix of emotions. He understood that his words struck harder than he intended.

"I shouldn't have said those things," he said to himself, his voice filled with regret. He understood the depth of Priya's pain and the vulnerability she had expressed during their conversation.

Overlooking the city below, as he drowned his sorrows as he kept drinking the beer. The scent of smoke filled the night air, as he reached for another cigarette, only to realize that the entire box was empty. Ajay rose from his chair, the alcohol impairing his balance. He leaned against the balcony railing and gazed up at the vast expanse of the night sky, where the stars twinkled with an ethereal beauty.

"You know Priya, he thought, I have seen people talk about the moon and the stars when they're in love, in our story I can completely resonate with that, because just like the moon, you are far away from me."

Tears filled Ajay's eyes, making it hard for him to see clearly as he pleaded for understanding. "I really love you Priya, I adore you so much. Do you even realise how much I care about you and how much I'm hurting?" he said

Ajay quickly wiped his tears as he heard a sudden knock on the door, his mother opened the door and stepped inside to invite him for the dinner but as she looked at the surroundings, she couldn't help but notice the bottles of beers lying around the floor. She could feel that Ajay's in some kind of a trouble.

"Ajay, what happened to you?" she asked, her voice trembling with worry and affection.

His emotions felt overwhelming, he turned his tear-stained face towards his mother. His voice broke as he struggled to find words. he walked towards her, his steps were unsteady, and embraced her tightly, seeking a sense of comfort. His mother, held him close to her.

Before she could say anything, Ajay's voice broke a bit as he tried to speak, "I... I don't want this marriage, mom." Tears started rolling from his eyes, He looked at his mother with tear filled eyes "Priya isn't happy with this marriage mom, it's better for us part ways from each other."

His mother's mind was filled with questions, she kept wondering why he would turn to alcohol to supress everything that bothered him. but among those question there was one that she couldn't find an answer to, why would he say that she's isn't happy with him?

She held his arm and took him to bed, she made sure he was comfortable, he quickly fell asleep. She overwhelmed by everything she saw. she knew that she would need some help to truly comprehend everything. She picked up her phone and dialled Rocky's number, he was the only person who could help Ajay.

"Hello?" Rocky said.

"Hi beta, I'm Ajay's mom, I hope I'm not disturbing you at this hour." She said.

"Hello aunty, not at all, is everything okay? he asked.

"Actually, I need your help, I feel Ajay's going through something and not trying to communicate, he hasn't been himself lately." She said

"I understand your concern, Auntie. You're right, Ajay has been a bit off lately. We've talked about a few things, but he hasn't opened up completely." he said.

"I appreciate your honesty, Rocky. It's just that as his mother, I'm worry about him. He's always been such a lively and cheerful person, but lately, he seems lost somehow." she said.

"I completely understand, I'm always there for him whenever he needs me." Rocky said

"Rocky, Would you be willing to come and see Ajay in person? I believe your presence could really make a difference." She said

"Absolutely, Auntie. I was just about to suggest the same thing. I'll be there in no time." he said

With that they disconnected the call, Rocky quickly got ready and stepped into his car.

Meanwhile, Shreya and Anjali sat at the dining table, eagerly waiting for Priya to join them for dinner. Anjali noticed that Priya was missing and grew concerned. She turned to her mom and asked, "Mom, Priya doesn't want to eat? Is everything okay?"

Her mom looked at her and said, "Priya isn't feeling well, she doesn't want to eat anything."

Anjali received a call from rocky, she excused herself and went to her room to answer it.

"Hey Anjali, I wanted to talk to you about Ajay." Rocky said.

"Hi Rocky. What's going on? Is everything okay with Ajay?" Anjali asked.

"I had a conversation with Ajay's mom. She's been worried about him lately, noticing that he's not himself. I have a feeling that Priya and Ajay still haven't resolved their underlying issues yet, in fact, his mom suggested that I should talk to him in person. I'll meet him today and then see how things turn out." Rocky said

"You should definitely meet him. I think it's important for Ajay to know that we're all here for him." Anjali said

"I told his mom that I'll be there in no time." Rocky said.

"Sounds good. Take care, Rocky." Anjali said.

"Yeah, We'll get through this together. See you soon." Rocky said.

They ended the call, leaving Anjali with a sense of relief that Rocky was taking the initiative to reach out to Ajay.

Meanwhile, Priya was in her room, Sitting on her bad and as usual recollected the events happened throughout the day. "I didn't expect him to behave like that " she thought. she was at her lowest, as if nothing could help her cope with her feelings, except for one thing – writing.

At some point we all feel that we don't have anyone to talk to – we feel like we have a bunch of stories brewing inside us but we don't find anyone who could listen to us silently. Whenever Priya felt the same, she would turn to her diary.

She looked around in her messy room, realizing how her emotions had affected her physical space. Books were scattered on the table, forgotten and disorganized. She noticed her diary amidst the clutter and picked it up.

She couldn't ignore the impact her emotional struggles had on her surroundings. The mess reflected the chaos she experienced internally, with no order or tranquillity left.

With each book put back in its place and each surface cleared, Priya felt a shift within. The physical space began to reflect her growing strength and resilience. Bringing order to her surroundings gave her clarity she needed at the moment.

She took her diary from the pile of books, she opened a blank page and then started writing, "You do know that I can't stay away from you, and yet there's this feeling that maybe distance is better for us — and that feeling won't fade away no matter how hard I try." She tapped her pen against her lips as if she was trying to gather some words.

"Each we met, I felt amazed by the amount of affecting you express, even without the words. she continued, as if our hearts have their own whispered ways of communicating with each other."

"We kissed in the rain today, for a moment everything faded away, it's been a while since I was craving for your touch, the way your lips touched against mine – was like a gentle reminder of our love. The rain continued to cascade around us, and the raindrops added their sweetness in the taste of your lips. That moment will stay with me forever."

Her thoughts were interrupted by a sudden knock on her door, Priya immediately closed her diary and put it aside. She opened the door and noticed that Anjali was standing against the door.

Both of them set on the bed, there was silence for a moment. as if Anjali was rehearsing her words before saying them.

"Priya, I wanted to talk to you." Anjali said.

"Yeah sure." Priya said.

"Did you guys talk things over? I assume everything should be okay at this point." Anjali said.

"Yes, we did." Priya said, she was still trying to comprehend the reason behind his behaviour – something she had experienced for the first time.

"Listen Priya, you do realise there's not much time left for your marriage, you can't just stay like that the whole time."

Priya looked down, her eyes filled with sadness and apprehension. She took a deep breath, summoning the courage to respond. please try to understand. This is not an easy decision for me.

Anjali was unable to contain her anger any longer, interrupts Priya, her voice filled with frustration. "Stop this nonsense, Priya! I'm tired of listening to these excuses for days now. You've been dragging this on, and it's driving me insane!"

Priya looked up, taken aback by Anjali's outburst. Tears started rolling out of her eyes as she struggles to find the right words to explain herself, but Anjali's anger remains unyielding. "Anjali, It's not about being selfish or unfair. This is about us three sisters," Priya said.

"Are you mad or what? You do know that Ajay was part of the past and we have moved on from that. Why don't you realise this one simple fact."

Priya's tears increase, her voice choked with emotion as she responds to Anjali's harsh words. "Yes, I am stupid. Yes, I am a fucking idiot. But, Anjali, my sister Shreya... she still loves Ajay. How can I snatch away her love?"

Priya's words flowed like a river, her words carrying the weight of her feelings. She revealed the difficulties, uncertainties, and unanswered questions that had been troubling her. Anjali gave Priya a place to express her feelings because she recognized the gravity of the situation.

"Priya, while I appreciate your concern for your sister, you cannot put your own happiness on the line for her sake. We've both moved on from Ajay, and you deserve to find love and happiness too," Anjali said.

"I know, Anjali, but Shreya was truly happy with him." Priya said.

"Priya, your words surpass my comprehension." Anjali said and walked out of the room. she headed towards the kitchen, poured herself a glass of water and took a deep breath. After calming herself down a bit she headed towards Shreya's room.

As she stepped inside Shreya's room, she noticed something interesting. Shreya sat on the sofa; her eyes fixed on the laptop screen. She was completely immersed in the movie. Anjali approached her cautiously, her concern evident in her voice.

"Shreya, I want to talk to you. Let's go out for a walk and have a conversation."

"Sure, Anjali. What's the matter? Is everything alright?" Shreya asked.

"It's something important." Anjali said

Shreya, sensing the seriousness in Anjali's voice, nodded in agreement. The two of them step out onto the road outside their house, joining the flow of people passing by. As they walk, Anjali takes a deep breath, gathering her thoughts. Just as she's about to speak, Shreya interrupted her.

"What's the matter? Tell me already." Shreya asked.

"Are you still in love with him?" Anjali asked.

Shreya's expressions changed as she heard those words, She took a breath and said, "Ajay and Priya are about to get married, Anjali. What are you saying?"

She reached out and placed a comforting hand on Shreya's shoulder. "I know, Shreya. but as your sister, it's my duty to ask you honestly about your feelings.

It's important for us to have open and truthful conversations."

Shreya was silent for a moment, lost in her thoughts, she was wondering if she should say the truth, she finally broke her silence, "Yes, I still have feelings for him," she said.

"Are you mad ? Do you even realise what you just said? your sister's future is at stake right now." Anjali's words hung heavy in the air, she suddenly stopped speaking. Tears welled up in her eyes, and her voice broke with vulnerability.

Shreya, taken aback by the raw emotions pouring out of her sister, looks at Anjali with a mix of guilt and sadness. "It's all my fault, I wish we never met."

Anjali started crying , her tears cascading down her cheeks. The weight of the truth hung heavily in the air, overshadowing their bond as sisters. "You should move on from the past Shreya, he's getting married with our sister, think about their future."

Shreya took a pause to comprehend how the past choices were affecting the present. "We need to fix this Shreya, He loves Priya and cares about her more than anything in the world, he didn't want to hide anything from her so he decided to share everything about his past relationships. Think about all this Shreya." Anjali said

Their conversation continued as they walked, their voices blending with the sounds of cars and the people passing by. Anjali was determined to help Priya, and she knew that Shreya's support was crucial.

Meanwhile, Ajay was asleep in his room when he heard the knock on the door, he woke up and opened the door.

Rubbing his eyes Ajay noticed that Rocky was standing outside the room, Hey, Rocky. "What brings you here? Did I fall asleep?" Ajay said

"Ajay, I'm really worried about you. Your mom called me and told me about everything, I wanted to talk to you in person." Rocky said.

Ajay could barely manage to stand on his own.

"We all have our low moments. But drowning your sorrows in alcohol won't solve anything. We need to talk, man. I want to understand what you're going through." Rocky said as he placed a hand on Ajay's Sholder.

"You're right, Rocky. I've been struggling with my thoughts about me and Priya. Things have gotten complicated, and I'm feeling lost. I don't know how to handle it all." Ajay said.

"I'm here for you, Ajay. Let's sit down and talk it out. Sometimes, sharing your feelings and getting another perspective can provide clarity. You don't have to face this alone, I'm always there to help you." Rocky said.

"Thanks, Rocky. I appreciate your support. I've been holding up so much inside, and it's been consuming me. I need to find some clarity." Ajay said.

"You can talk about it, buddy; that's the only way we'll be able to make sense of this. Please feel free to express your thoughts. Rocky said.

"There are a lot of things to discuss, but I never thought that the decisions I made in the past would completely alter the course of my life. I'm beginning to think that we were never meant to be in each other's lives." Ajay said

"I understand but I feel like you guys are made for each other, I have seen the affection you feel for her, I know that even if she were to deny the idea of marriage you wouldn't blame her, in fact you love her so much that you are willing to push yourself to the boundaries just so you could be with her." Rocky said

"I know, but she wouldn't think that way; buddy, I'm the one who caused all the trouble; I don't deserve to be in her life. I thought being honest was the right thing to do, but it seems to have caused more confusion and doubt." Ajay said

"I understand, Ajay. But being honest is the best thing you could do in a relationship; you haven't done anything wrong. In fact, it allows both of you to truly understand each other." Rocky said

"You're right Rocky, But at this point I feel guilty for sharing those details and making her feel so hurt and confused." Ajay said

"Ajay, We all experience the highs and lows of relationships. But it's how you handle those situations, that's what matters. I feel that communication is the key, talk to her, tell her everything you think about, I'm sure she'd understand." Rocky said

"You're right, Rocky. I need to have a conversation with her, to bridge the gap that has formed between us. I want her to understand that my past doesn't define the person I am today or how I feel about her."

"Remember Ajay, Priya loves you and deserves a man who will take good care of her. you have done the right thing by expressing her the truth about the past relationships." Rocky said

"Thanks for being here, Rocky. Your words and perspective mean a lot to me." Ajay said

"I'm here for you, Ajay. I believe in you both" Rocky said

A smile emerged on Ajay's face, as if a ray of hope striking through the thick clouds, his burdened heart feeling lighter after the heartfelt conversation with Rocky. The weight of his worries began to fade, replaced by a new sense of positivity and resolve.

Ajay looked at the window, and there was a silhouette of some kind, face wasn't quite clear, Ajay and rocky sat there enveloped in the silence of the room. his eyes fixated on faint silhouette of a figure, gradually it became quite vivid and there was a sense of familiarity. The dim glow from the distant streetlamp highlighted the figure's outline but kept its identity a secret.

What do you think about this Rocky? Ajay asked as his heart was racing.

Rocky's eyes remained fixed on the window, "I'm not sure, Ajay. It's strange, though. Who could be standing out there at this hour?" he said

Ajay stood up from the bed, Ajay gradually walked towards the window, the stood there without moving, as if waiting for them to move closer. The night air was thick with anticipation as Ajay tried to approach her.

A gust of wind rustled the nearby trees, creating a shadow that allowed the figure to remain hidden.

Ajay was close to the figure, he tried to reach the handle of the shutter to slide it open and then as soon as he opened the window, the figure ran away, he shouted but his voice wasn't reachable.

Her identity remained a mystery except for one thing that Ajay noticed, he saw that the figure was wearing a hoodie and because of the wind the cap flung opened revealing the glossy hair with a hair band on them.

"It was a girl." Ajay said.

Rocky remained silent as he was wondering what just happened.

Amidst all that, the question remained unanswered: Who was she?

Book 7: Everlasting Love

Chapter – 13

July 2023, 1 Week Before Marriage

Anjali, Priya, and Shreya gathered in Priya's living room, enjoying their chilled beers as they settled into a relaxed atmosphere. The room was filled with the sound of their laughter and the clinking of glasses, setting the stage for a deep conversation that was about to take place.

"You know, it feels so good to spend an evening like this, just the three of us." Anjali said as she took a sip from her drink.

Priya nodded, "You're right. Life has been so busy lately, and I've missed these kinds of moments with you guys."

Shreya took a moment to gather her thoughts and said, "Priya, we really care about you but we have noticed that you've been holding onto the past. It's time for you to detach yourself from the past and think about your future with him."

Priya's thought about the past as she heard those words, "I understand what you're saying but I feel it's not for me to simply let go of everything."

"You have to take the step Priya. you deserve all the love and happiness that awaits you." Shreya said

Anjali reached out and gently placed a hand on Priya's shoulder, "Priya, we understand that it's not easy. But you deserve someone like Ajay, someone who has constantly made an effort to be in your life. Think about all those beautiful moments you shared, It's worth giving it another chance."

Shreya nodded in agreement, "Priya, we've seen the incredible affection he feels for you and the bond you share with Ajay. It's undeniable. But holding onto the past can prevent us from embracing the future and the happiness that awaits us," she said

Shreya finished her beer bottle and said in a lower tone, "Ajay has shown his commitment and genuine concern for you. He really loves you and I know that you guys can build a new future together."

"I really appreciate your words Shreya, but what if everything falls apart?" Priya said

Shreya was silent for a while, she knew that she had feelings for him but at the moment she had to put everything aside and focus on the situation at hand,

"Priya, she continued as she gradually tried to make an eye contact, he was part of my past." she said putting the weight on the "was" word. I know that I had feelings for him but I have moved on from there, you deserve him more than anything else in the world, I know it took me long to say this but I have come to the conclusion that our story was meant to remain incomplete."

Shreya paused, and took a deep breath.

"Shreya, whenever I think about you and him together, It evokes a storm of emotions inside of me. sometimes it strikes a chord within me as those pictures flash in front of eyes, each moment feels like a constant battle between past and present." Priya said

"It's okay to feel that way, I too feel like why we crossed our paths but I can never change the past right? moving on is the only choice I had." Shreya said

Anjali reached out and clasped Priya's hand, her touch warm and reassuring, "Remember Priya, this is a new chapter of your life, a chance to build something beautiful with Ajay. You deserve to be happy, to experience a love that fulfils you in every way."

Shreya brought another bottle of beer while Anjali and Priya sat in silence, Shreya settled in the couch and said, "Ajay has shown his dedication and genuine care for you. Don't let the fear of what might happen stop you from experiencing a love that could be everything you've ever wanted."

Priya listened intently, her eyes searching Shreya's face for any signs of doubt. She took a deep breath, contemplating Shreya's words.

"Shreya, you're right. Ajay has proven time and again that he is willing to put in the effort, to fight for our relationship. I know that no matter what happens in life, he'll always be there for me."

Anjali leaned in and said in her warm voice "Priya, we believe in you. We've seen the way you two connect, the way you bring out the best in each other. We're always there for you."

Anjali and Shreya shared a proud smile, their support unwavering. They understood that this was Priya's journey, and they were there to guide her through it. Together, they continued to delve deeper into their conversation. Priya smiled appreciatively, feeling a surge of gratitude for her sister's relentless support. Their words started to resonate deep within her, gradually soothing her worries.

Priya raised her beer glass, "To love and taking chances," she said, her voice filled with determination. Anjali and Shreya clinked their glasses against hers. Each moment seemed to strengthen the bond they shared.

Priya was grateful to be surrounded by people who deeply cared about her. She knew that her worries wouldn't fade away overnight, but gradually they would.

The night grew darker, the three of them set in silence embracing the bond they shared, their beer bottles were empty, As they looked at each other, a soft smile emerged on Priya's lips.

Anjali broke the silence, "Well, I think it's safe to say that we've solved all of the world's problems tonight, over a few beers."

"Of course! Who knew that this evening would turn into a therapy session?" Shreya said

Priya could finally feel a sense of happiness brewing inside her, as if the conversation gave her the perspective she wanted, she was now anticipating the good things in her life.

They continued to enjoy each other's company, the conversation flowing effortlessly between them. They celebrated the present, embracing the laughter and the comfort that came with it.

The room fell into silence again, the night grew darker the shining stars illuminated the sky. Shreya adjusted her pillow on the sofa and gradually fell asleep.

Anjali whispered trying not to interrupt her sleep, " I guess our night owl does need some sleep."

Priya tried to contain her laughter, as she looked at Anjali.

"Take some rest Priya," Anjali said, "I too need some sleep."

"Good night, Anjali."

"Good night, Priya."

Anjali went to her room, she turned of the night lamp and fall asleep, meanwhile Priya brough her diary from her room and set on the sofa close to Shreya, she couldn't help but smile at her.

She opened a fresh blank page and started writing, "I guess now I can give words to my feelings, to be honest, I feel empty with you."

She paused for a while to collect her thoughts.

"I have felt the affection you feel for me, I know how you keep putting efforts to be in my life, I know that I should accept your past as a part of your life, I guess more than anything I miss being with you, I can't imagine how happy it would be to wake up next to you, I cannot wait to experience the moment when we would take a walk alongside the river while the starry sky would illuminate our surroundings and your presence would make things more magical. I often find myself reflecting on the moments I shared with you – something in your presence makes me forget about the world."

Priya placed the pen in the diary and closed it, and in a moment she fell asleep. The weight of her emotions eased, as she found her comfort in the written words.

The next morning, she woke up and noticed that she fell sleep on the sofa, she looked around to see that

Shreya was still asleep. She couldn't help but smile at her. she checked her phone and noticed a notification of a WhatsApp message; it was from Ajay. A sense of happiness washed over her as she unlocked her phone to read his message.

"Hey Priya! I feel really grateful to have someone like you in my life, I want you to know that my love for you is everlasting. I really want to apologise for all the pain and confusion you went through. You bring so much happiness in my life, I want to be with you – forever. I promise you that I would stay with you in any and every situation of life. Love, Ajay."

Priya instantly typed a response "I can't wait to be with you too, I know that everything that happened has only increased more confusion in our life, but not anymore, I want to embrace my present which is of course you. Love you, can't wait to see you."

The words she typed conveyed her deep affection for Ajay, and she couldn't help but smile at the thought of their connection growing stronger with each passing day.

Priya's fingers hovered over her phone, the urge to call him becoming almost irresistible. Yet, a hesitation gripped her, whispering doubts and uncertainties into her mind. Maybe it's not the right time, she thought. Maybe I should wait a little longer.

She ignored her longing and focused on her daily activities, looking for comfort in the routine. Her worries were washed away by the shower's warm water, and when she got out, she carefully chose her favourite dress from her wardrobe. She looked at herself in the mirror and smiled softly. She felt a sense of anticipation at the thought of him seeing her in this outfit.

There was an urge she couldn't resist, Filled with a mix of excitement and nervousness, she grabbed her phone turned the camera towards the mirror posing herself for a picture. And she captured a beautiful picture of herself in her favourite outfit. She looked at the picture over and over, should I share it with him? she thought, and then she finally decided to send the picture. Priya couldn't help but wonder how he would react. Would he appreciate the gesture? Would it reignite something between them?

Ajay's heart skipped a beat as he eagerly unlocked his phone to check the photo she had sent. A rush of emotions washed over him as he kept looking at the picture, she looked confident in her favourite outfit which instantly captivated him.

With a sense of excitement, He typed his response, "You look absolutely stunning! That outfit suits you perfectly."

He instantly opened the contact list and called her, His heart raced, anticipation and nervousness intertwining within him. finally, Priya's voice filled his ears.

"Hello?" Priya answered carrying a sense of surprise as she didn't expect him to instantly call her.

"Hey, Priya," Ajay said, "I just had to call you after seeing that photo. You look absolutely beautiful."

"Thank you, Ajay. I wasn't sure if I should have sent it, but I'm glad I did." Priya said

"I'm glad you did," Ajay said in a softer tone. "It reminded me of how special you are to me. It made me realize how much I miss you, Priya."

Priya's voice trembled slightly as she responded, "I've missed you too, Ajay. There's so much I want to say, but I feel like I don't have the words for it."

"Priya, I want to be there for you and support you in any and every situation." Ajay said.

Priya's voice softened, "I want that too, Ajay. I want us to find our way back to each other, to rediscover the love and affection we once had."

Ajay took a moment to collect his words, "There's something I want to say to you Priya."

Priya felt a sense of worry about what he might say, "What is it, Ajay? please tell me."

"Even in the moments when we were apart, I never stopped thinking about you Priya, I feel like I can't imagine my life without you. I have come to realise that even in the difficult times my love for you only grew stronger." Ajay said

Priya felt a surge of happiness within her, "Ajay... I've felt the same way. Even through the pain and confusion, my love for you never faded. It's always been there with me."

"Priya, will you give us another chance? Let's rebuild what we had, stronger than ever," Ajay said a sense of venerability could be felt in his voice.

Priya's heart was blooming with a sense of happiness and joy, "Yes, Ajay. I want that too, let's give our love the chance it deserves."

Their voices blended in a symphony of love, as they poured their hearts out, expressing their desires and dreams. Even through the ups and downs of life, their love for each other never faded.

Meanwhile, as Ajay and Priya were engaged in their heartfelt conversation, their families were bustling with energy and excitement, ensuring that all the preparations for the upcoming wedding were meticulously taken care of.

Priya's mother was carefully checking the arrangements in one corner of the house, making sure that every decoration was placed precisely. She was dressed in a vibrant saree. Her eyes sparkled with happiness as she imagined her daughter being happy and looked forward to the joining of two families.

Ajay's mother was busy working with the caterers to make sure the menu reflected the mouthwatering dishes that would leave a lasting impression on the guests.

Outside, in the apartment garden, the wedding mandap stood tall and majestic, adorned with fragrant flowers and intricate decorations.

The aroma of freshly prepared foods spread through the air as the sun started to set, casting a warm golden glow over the.

In the days that followed, amidst the chaos of wedding planning, Ajay and Priya stole some moments to talk over a phone call or texts, they found joy in sharing the funny incidents that happened throughout the busy days.

Often their conversations would take a romantic turn, effortlessly reminding each other of the depth of their love and the desire they felt to be in each other's arms.

They would think back on their journey together, recalling special moments and imagining the wonderful future that lay ahead of them.

They would often talk until late night, looking at the stary sky, Ajay had a habit of saying that he could compare her with the stars and moon, but they would feel shy just by looking at her, Every time he said this, Priya would laugh out loud and eventually tell him how much she loved talking to him.

July 2023, A Day Before Marriage

Finally, the day of the Haldi ceremony arrived. The air was filled with excitement and joy as the house was adorned with yellow decorations, symbolizing the auspicious occasion. Family members and close friends gathered, all dressed in shades of vibrant yellow.

Ajay's and Priya's families busily prepared for the rituals, meticulously arranging the traditional elements. Bowls filled with Haldi paste, fragrant oils, and flowers were delicately placed on a table.

Ajay was dressed in an elegant Yellow kurta, was escorted by his friends and family to the Haldi area. His radiant smile reflected the happiness that radiated from his heart.

Meanwhile, Priya, adorned in a vibrant yellow saree, was surrounded by her loved ones, Everyone got ready for the joyful ceremony of covering the bride in Haldi paste. her family members gathered to shower her with love and well wishes, The bright yellow Haldi paste was amusingly applied to her cheeks, hands, and arms to symbolise the blessings of the upcoming wedding.

The stage was adorned with vibrant decorations and a beautiful sofa where Priya and Ajay sat, adorned in their yellow attire perfectly complementing the ceremony theme. Their parents joined her on the stage, their smiles reflecting their joy and pride. The photographer captured the candid moments of their togetherness.

Priya's mother smiled brightly as she looked at Priya, "Oh, look at our beautiful bride! It's finally your Haldi ceremony, my dear."

"Thank you, Mom. I can't believe the day is finally here." Priya said as she smiled at her mother.

"Look at that radiant smile, Priya. It seems like you're the happiest person in the room." Priya's father playfully teased her.

"Thank you, dad. I'm so grateful to have you by my side," Priya laughed.

Priya's mother tenderly applied Haldi on her face, "Today we're showering you with our love and blessings for a bright and blissful future."

"Thank you, Mom. Your love and support mean everything to me. I'm lucky to have you by my side," Priya had tears In her eyes but she calmed herself down.

"You're embarking on a new journey, my princess. Remember, no matter where life takes you, we'll always be there for you, cheering you on and guiding you along the way." Her father said as he gently caressed her head.

"Dad. Your words give me strength and courage. I'm filled with so much gratitude and love right now."

In that moment, she knew that she was surrounded by the unconditional love and support of her parents, ready to embrace the new chapter of her life.

Amidst all the happiness and excitement, Priya and Ajay stole moments to look at each other, often times they would make an eye contact without saying a word. It felt as if what they felt for each other couldn't be conveyed in a combination of few phrases – it was ineffable.

As relatives and friends eagerly came up on stage to apply Haldi on Ajay, he couldn't help but notice that Rocky hadn't yet applied any Haldi on him yet. He looked around in the crowed of his relatives and finally caught a glimpse of rocky playfully dodging the crowd, trying to make his way towards Ajay.

"Hey Rocky! Come here and join in the Haldi ceremony" Ajay said.

"Haha, I'm on my way, Ajay! Can't miss out on it bro. It's time to get all yellowed up! Rocky said.

Rocky went on stage, he took a flower from the table and gently applied some Haldi on Ajay's face.

"Rocky, you sure know how to make an entrance! I was wondering where you were hiding." Ajay laughed.

"Haha, sorry for the delay buddy, anyways congratulations to both of you." Rocky said

"Thank you, I'm glad you made it even special for me with your presence." Ajay said

"Always there, buddy," Rocky said.

He clicked some photographs with Ajay and Priya, he shook hands at the end congratulating them for the new beginnings of their life.

As the Haldi ceremony unfolded, bringing with it a sense of anticipation and joy. It served as a gateway to the grand celebrations that lay ahead. It was a reminder of the love and blessings that surrounded them, setting the stage for a beautiful and everlasting union.

Shreya and Anjali found a moment to converse as everyone was busy clicking pictures of the couple.

"Anjali, look at Priya, she looks absolutely stunning in her yellow saree, doesn't she?" Shreya said.

"I know Shreya, it's such a beautiful moment for both of them, I'm so happy for them." Anjali said.

"Yeah, she's lucky to have someone who truly cares for her." Shreya said

"I feel the same way, Shreya." Anjali said

Priya called them on stage so she could click a picture with them.

Shreya and Anjali joined Priya on the stage, standing by her side as they posed for the photograph. They wrapped their arms around each other, sharing a genuine smile filled with love and joy.

The ceremony brought together cherished traditions and deep emotions among the guests. It represented the fusion of two souls, a celebration of their love and the promising future they would have together.

The cameras clicked some candid pictures, freezing those precious moments of the occasion, ensuring that the memories would be cherished for a lifetime.

Sun was gradually fading behind the clouds, the family members started to wrap up the Haldi ceremony. Later on, they beautifully decorated hall, adorned with colourful drapes and twinkling lights. The air was filled with excitement as they prepared for the much-awaited sangeet ceremony.

The stage was beautifully decorated at the centre of the garden, adorned with flowers and shimmering decorations, ready to host the captivating performances of the evening.

Guests arrived one by one, dressed in their finest clothing, bringing with them an aura of joy and celebration.

The night unfolded with a spectacular combination of music and dance. Each performance was filled passion and precision, captivating the guests. the stage came alive with vibrant colours of lights.

Priya, dressed in a stunning traditional outfit, took the stage for a special performance. Her radiant smile and graceful moves captured the hearts of everyone present. All the guests gave her a round of applauds after her stunning performance.

She looked at Ajay, who was standing next to Rocky close to the stage as she caught her breath. She held out her hand, inviting him to join her on stage.

Ajay was surprised by the unexpected invitation, he hesitated for a moment. But the enthusiasm and happiness in her eyes compelled him forward. he held her hand as she walked down a few steps to invite him over the stage, he stepped onto the stage, his heart racing with anticipation.

Priya guided Ajay through a few basic dance steps, what mattered the most in that moment was the connection they shared, which was enough to create magic on the stage.

The cheers and whistles from the guests intensified as they realised how much love and affection was truly being expressed through their performance.

Priya took a moment to catch her breath, "Ajay, that was amazing."

Ajay smiled at her as he too was slightly out of breath "I couldn't have done it without you."

"Oh, come on, we were in perfect sync, as if we've been dancing together forever," Priya said.

"I couldn't take my eyes off you. You looked absolutely stunning, Priya," Ajay said.

"Thank you, Ajay. But it was your presence that made it special," Priya said.

Their conversation was interrupted by the applause and cheers from the guests, a response to the magic they had just created on stage. soon the final notes of music faded away and the sangeet ceremony came to an end. The family members exchanged heartfelt embraces.

Chapter – 14

18 July 2023, Marriage Day

Finally, the marriage day arrived, the day she had been waiting for finally arrived. The day when the love would untie two souls for a bond that would transcend the borders of time itself.

The venue was beautifully decorated, with flowers adorning every corner, it emanated an aura of serenity and beauty.

Priya was happy as the thought of being with him crossed her mind, she felt a sense of excitement as she envisioned herself as his wife, she imagined her daily life with him, each moment filled with love and affection, even the daily boring tasks would be magical in his presence. she was sitting Infront of a mirror smiling at her reflection, she was adorned in a beautiful attire for the wedding day.

Ajay, the groom, appeared stunning in his professionally tailored sherwani. As he looked at his reflection in the mirror, thoughts of Priya filled his mind, A beautiful sense of anticipation washed over him as he was about to marry the love of his life. the person who held the key to his happiness. Her radiant smile, her gentle touch, everything about her made him happy.

Guests began to arrive. They took their seats with the anticipation for the marriage rituals to begin. The melodious tunes of traditional wedding music filled the air, making the ambience even more magical.

Ajay sat on the chair designated for the groom, he was nervous and excited at the same time while he eagerly waited for her to arrive. each moment felt like an eternity while he waited for the moment when he would catch a glimpse of his bride.

After what it felt like an eternity, the moment Ajay was waiting for had arrived. Priya made her way down the aisle accompanied by her loved ones, all eyes were fixated on her, the photographers captured each step she took – freezing moments of time so the bride and groom can cherish them for the times to come.

Ajay stood there looking at her, he couldn't help but think about how beautiful she was looking. She came closer and their eyes met, a smile emerged on everyone's face as they witness the beautiful couple radiating love and affection for each other.

The pandit began the sacred rituals, speaking verses to seek blessings from the divine, The flame of the wedding rituals burned bright, symbolizing the strong and eternal bond they shared.

Ajay and Priya stood by the sacred flames with their hands entangled as they prepared for the Mangal

Phera ritual that would bind them together. the pandit chanted the sacred mantras, guiding them through the ritual. The happiness in the air was almost tangible as their loved ones were showering flowers on the beautiful bride and groom. After completing each round, they exchanged heartfelt glances, conveying their love and affection.

After completing the first round of Mangal Phera Priya spoke a Sanskrit verse, her voice reverberated in the air.

तीर्थव्रतोद्यापन यज्ञकर्म मया सहैव प्रियवयं कुर्या:।

वामांगमायामि तदा त्वदीयं ब्रवीति वाक्यं प्रथमं कुमारी॥

"May I perform sacred pilgrimages, fasts, and sacrificial rites with you, my beloved, as my partner. From this day forward, I promise to be on your left side, uttering this vow as a maiden."

A silence filled the air as people heard the verse. It created an atmosphere of cheerfulness and amusement among the guests.

Ajay looked at her and asked, "Do you know Sanskrit?

Priya smiled, "I have a basic understanding of the language, but I may make some errors in the precise translations."

They continued the Mangal Phera ritual as per pandits guidance and Amidst the chanting of mantras and the showering of flower petals, the couple was pronounced husband and wife.

Ajay looked at her and said, "I promise you that each and every moment of your life would be filled with the love and happiness."

"I promise you, that I will stay by your side in any and every situation of life." Priya said

"Even in the difficult times, my love for you will never fade." Ajay said

"I believe in us, Ajay, I know we will find the light even in the darkest times of our life." Priya said.

A joyful cheer erupted among the guests, excitement filled the air as they showered the couple with vibrant petals and fragrant flowers.

Shreya sat alone in her room, completely absorbed in a book. Outside, she could hear the sounds of laughter and chatter from the cheerful guests at the wedding. As the last part of the ceremony, the "Vidaai" took place, the noise grew softer. Shreya remained immersed in the pages of her book.

After a while of reading a few pages, she placed a bookmark so she could continue to engage with words right at the point she stopped. She put down her book and looked out of the window, the happiness of the newly married couple was almost tangible, people were giving them the blessing as they were about to begin a new chapter of their life.

Her eyes were focused on him, the person she fell in love with in her collage days, "I wanted to surprise you on that day when I came to your place but when I saw that you too were entangled in your own issues, I stayed at the window and kept looking at you."

"Our story was purely romantic, just like the ones I read In novels. It had words, perhaps a lot of them, but we never realised how some chapters still remain unwritten; our story didn't end like the ones in novels. Perhaps there's a similarity between both real life and novels—you never know how things unfold."

Special Thanks

Jatin Solanki

Epilogue

A Month Later

Late in the night, Priya and Ajay were standing at the balcony of a hotel in goa, overlooking the beautiful beach and the moonlit surroundings. The gentle waves crashing against the shore created a magical symphony that enveloped the two of them in the tranquil ambience.

"The beach looks beautiful at night, doesn't it?" She asked.

"It does actually, but not as mesmerising as you, your presence itself is captivating." He said as he looked at her.

She blushed, "do you really think so?"

"I do. You look like a poetry to me and each time I look at you, your eyes steal my words away." He said.

"Thank you for making me feel this way, I love the way you think about me." She said.

Their hands entwined, telling a series of stories that formed the love they shared.

"It feels like we just met yesterday and fell in love and now we are together sharing this beautiful view." he said.

"Come to think of it, I too feel the same way, everything happened in an instant, like a sudden blow of wind that changed the course of our fate, bringing us together so we can share the same future." she said.

"You know, the idea of waking up next to you feels like a dream come true." he said

"I'm forever grateful to be here with you, I too feel like I'm living my dream." She said

They watched the waves dancing in the moonlight and the soft wind played with their hairs.

The next morning, Priya and Ajay were walking on the beach with their hands entwined, soaking in the cool breeze, the tranquil beach came alive as the morning sun painted the water with its golden hues creating a captivating scenario.

"The beach is beautiful, Isn't it." Priya said

"Yeah, but your presence makes it more magical." Ajay said

Priya smiled, "This beach, freshness of this morning, you and me everything seems perfect."

"It's more than perfect Priya, it is the most beautiful moment of my life." Ajay said

The soft, golden sand caressed their feet, as they walked, savouring the tranquillity of the moment. Ajay quickly wrapped his arms around her waist, and lifted her off her feet. She wrapped her arms around his neck, feeling safe and happy in his embrace. The two of them laughed as they soaked in each other's affection.

After a while, they sat on the golden sand, their bodies close, their faces only inches apart. Ajay leaned in and pressed his lips against Priya's. they shared a gentle kiss, conveying their love, trust, and the magic of the moment. The world around them seemed to fade away as they lost themselves in the connection they shared.

Meanwhile, Anjali and rocky were sitting at the Riverfront in Ahmadabad, looking over to the ripples of the water, it felt like the river had some kind of ability to take their worries away and make them feel better.

"You know, I feel a little jealous of Ajay, I can't wait for us to be together and share those wonderful moments as a couple." Rocky said

"Now that you mention it, I do feel the same way. but sadly, we can't do anything about it right now. I too have dreamed about being with you but we have to keep In mind that everything happens at the right time." Anjali said, her eyes fixated on the flowing water.

"You are right, I know that we have been through so many things. I sometimes wonder if we would be able to handle challenges as Ajay and Priya did." Rocky said

Anjali leaned in closer, "Rocky, every relationship has its own unique set of challenges. What matters is how we face them together. We've seen Ajay and Priya's journey and the difficulties they went through, but used those difficulties to grow as a couple."

Rocky contemplated on her words, He gently held her hand and said, "Anjali, you have always been my compass, pointing me in the right direction during life's storms. Together we've faced so many challenges, and I have seen your strength in the tough times of your life. I know that with you by my side, we can overcome any difficulties that may arise."

"I think the best part is that everything happened as per our plan." Rocky said

"Yeah, although things went a little off course, everything ended up working in our favour."

"But, on second thoughts, I wonder what if everything falls apart? what if Ajay and Priya won't be there for us? Rocky said, he looked a bit worried

Anjali remained lost in thoughts, struggling to find the right words. in the midst of that, she kept looking at the vibrant colours of the sky, her mind drifted back to the moment they first met, even at the moment she could vividly imagine those times.

About The Author

As emerging authors Jiya and Joy Sengal brings a unique perspective in the fiction world. Their novel immerses us in an unforgettable love story that unfolds between the pages.

Throughout the book they're weaving a story that not only captivates us but also explores emotions of love and affection. Their vivid description of places allows us to immerse in the story and evokes strong emotions.

Using relatable characters, they breathe life into the story. They have their flaws which makes them easy to connect with. As we journey alongside the characters, we become emotionally invested in their world.

www.ingramcontent.com/pod-product-compliance
Lightning Source LLC
LaVergne TN
LVHW061609070526
838199LV00078B/7226